Jamie Pond
In
Rise Of The
Heron

By D.P. Hall

COPYRIGHT PROTECTION WARNING

The author has registered this work at ProtectMyWork.com

ISBN-13: 978-1539524168

ISBN-10:1539524167

For Julie, Kayleigh, Jack and Amy.

And in loving memory of Granny

Jamie Pond In Rise Of The Heron

CONTENTS

Jamie Pond In Rise Of The Heron

ACKNOWLEDGMENTS

A Great big thank you to my family for inspiring me to write this book and many more to come. Without their encouragement and understanding through hard times and good, I could not have done it.

Thanks again to my wife Julie and three children for believing in me and helping to make my dream come true of being a published Author.

Thank you to my editor, Sheryl Lee for working with me on Jamie Pond's first adventure.

http://sherylleee.wixsite.com/editor

CHAPTER 1 - JAMIE POND

There he was, our hero Special Agent Jamie Pond, standing at the edge of his large green country lily pad and staring at his reflection in the cool and calm waters of the lake he liked to call home.

"Looking good," he winked at his wavy reflection, which was rubbing a smooth green hand over an equally smooth green face.

It was six in the morning, and fresh dew sparkled in beams of warm orange sunlight as the sun's rays passed through gaps in the branches of the beech trees surrounding Jamie's lake. Jamie basked in the warm orange sunbeams, listening to the harmony of his fellow frogs and keeping one eye half open, ready to launch his sticky long tongue at the next unsuspecting fly. He lay on his lily pad for a few moments, drifting back to sleep, unaware of the dark shadowy figure rising out of the water. Jamie shivered. Although a cold shiver wasn't unusual for a cold-blooded frog, he was trying to enjoy the sun's warm rays and the sudden cold disturbed him for a second or two.

Red, a channel catfish and Jamie's best friend, stared into Jamie's face with one big bulbous eye only a few millimeters away and almost touching him. Jamie slowly opened both eyes, half-expecting rain clouds drawing in on him. Instead, he yelped at the sight of the big bulbous eye and long slippery whiskers invading his personal space. Startled, he jumped up from his slumber and without thinking posed in full Kung Fu stance ready to strike at the big bulbous eye.

"Red, I nearly took you out right there and then," Jamie shouted, catching his breath.

"Aw, give me a break Jamie, Agent Cod needs to see you right away," Red replied.

Agent Cod was the team leader of a secret government agency called The C.F.I.A. (Carp and Frog Intelligence Agency). They have led the fight against evil for nearly seventeen generations of elite frogs. The very best speckled tree frogs and giant toads train the C.F.I.A. agents.

Jamie is chief of Sector 'S' and has held this position for two years now.

Jamie has seen things in his two-year term at the agency that we could not even imagine.

Red, on the other hand, has only been in the spy business for just a few months. After graduation, Red took a break from the training academy and didn't want to rush into becoming a secret agent. He wanted to spend a bit more time with his family before moving away to Tilgate. Jamie and Red had become very close in the training academy, to the point of being the very best of friends.

"Do we have another pond to save?" Jamie asked Red.

"No, it's Cod," Red tried to answer.

Jamie interrupted. "A terrorist ready to take over the canal."

"No, it's......" Red continued and was interrupted again.

"I Know, I've got it! The Heron has just started another new organisation. He wants to take over the world and has built himself an underwater base off the South coast of England," Jamie said jokingly.

"Well," Red paused for a moment, contemplating the little information he actually knew, but then carried on.

"No, it's Cod and he wants his morning tea," Red said more gravely. Jamie's tea making skills were known all over the world!

Deep inside the west bank of the lake, there lay a hidden cavern. The cavern was only accessible from underwater and guarded by two of the meanest looking pikes Jamie had ever seen, and Jamie had seen a few in his time. The cavern hid the entrance to the secret headquarters of the C.F.I.A., set deep beneath the silt lake within a park called Tilgate Park just outside of Crawley in West Sussex, England. The Park gave the special agents the perfect cover for hiding from any undetected foe in the area and overhead surveillance spy drones.

Jamie perched at the edge of his lily pad and took one step back, then raised his arm ready for a perfect triple somersault into the water. Red bobbed up and down and rolled his eyes at his over the top friend.

With almost no splash or waves behind them, Jamie and Red swam down into the dark depths of the lake toward the entrance of the cavern. They took care to avoid the water nymphs and stickle- backs since they do hurt if you swim into one. Jamie shivered again as they descended into the dark depths of the lake. Soon they were deep in the silt beds where the sun couldn't reach them and nothing grew. Not even algae. Cautiously they approached the caverns entrance, trying not to disturb the guards.

Grumpy pair of fish, Jamie thought.

One of the pike guards, called Victor, shot out in front of them and shouted, "And just where do you think you two are going?"

The other pike floated near the entrance, growling and sneering at the unlikely heroes.

"Oh great, they heard us." Jamie screwed his nose up at the thought of being slapped in the face by wet fish.

Red jeered at the growling pikes, "Leave it out big gills."

"Watch it bait boy," Victor replied.

"Look, Victor, is that your name? Are you going to let us pass or not?" Jamie demanded.

"Oh, sorry boss I didn't recognise you there. In you go, Agent J," Victor said in his deep butch voice.

Jamie slipped past the gruesome twosome leaving Red to try to find his way past also. Hugo, the other pike, joined his scaly green friend and blocked the entrance to the headquarters, sniggering.

"I say again, leave it out big gills," Red demanded, with his long whiskers waving around in the gentle movement of the lake.

Victor and Hugo pushed back the pondweed hiding the entrance to headquarters. There was a sudden burst of light from within and Jamie and Red snapped their eyes shut at the blinding burst.

"Oh, great, all I can see now is a great big white spot in my eyes. Brilliant," Red moaned at Jamie.

The heroes swam cautiously through the long maze of tunnels, frequently blinded by more flashing lights from the walls as they swam.

"You know, Red, it doesn't matter how often I come down here. I will never get used to those two brutes at the entrance, and why does Cod insist on having cameras and strobe lights every couple of metres?" Jamie groaned.

After a few metres of flashes, white spots in their eyes and getting tangled up in pondweed, they reached a big shiny steel door. It looked like a large safe door holding back an enormous mountain of treasure. In the centre were two flashing glass panels. One was the shape of a hand and the other a fish's fin. Jamie placed his right hand on the respective panel and likewise Red.

A quiet female voice spoke. "Welcome, Agents J and R. Please swim back a bit to allow the door to open. We don't want any trapped fins or fingers now, do we."

Both Jamie and Red swam back a little bit and waited while the door whirred into action.

Clunk, clunk the gears strained as the door lifted.

"Quick Red, let's swim through before it slams shut on us," Jamie said hurriedly.

BANG

CRASH

The door slammed behind them, causing a swell in the water that shoved them into the opposite wall, facing the entrance they had just come through.

The not so quiet voice spoke again, "**Hold your positions.**"

Jamie and Red waited patiently as the water started to drain out of the chamber. The walls of the chamber were as dark and dingy as the maze of tunnels they had just swum through. On the back of the door and the facing wall there was the emblem of the C.F.I.A. Printed within the emblem was a picture of Cod. The picture was supposed to change with each new director. This picture had yet to change.

Red panicked a little, as he always did when the water from the chamber drained to reveal a grated platform. Red's fins and flippers were flying everywhere. His flapping calmed down a bit after a few moments when the water was at a level where Jamie could stand but keep Red just under water enough so he wouldn't drown. Flashing amber lights whirled in a frenzy at one corner of the platform. Jamie and Red both tutted and squinted their eyes again at the bright flashing light. The platform then jolted and descended deep into headquarters.

CHAPTER 2 - SPECIAL AGENT COD & THE C.F.I.A

"Ah, there you are J. Did you have a lie in this morning? I'm waiting for my cup of tea and you know you make the best tea this side of Crawley," Cod boomed in his firm voice.

During Jamie's training academy days, his instructors gave him the tea duties. They had soon discovered his awesome tea, and as Cod had said, he did make the best tea this side of Crawley.

Agent Cod was not a codfish as his name might suggest. He was the fattest, largest, and ugliest common carp fish of his kind. He didn't want to be associated with something as common as a carp fish because he liked to think he was posh. But deep down under that battle-scarred body, he was just a carp.

Director Cod had been in charge since the very beginning of the C.F.I.A. and had seen more agent J's come and go than he cared to remember. Many frogs were courageous and some were just plain stupid. There were a few that were perfect like our hero Special Agent Jamie Pond.

Cod, being the dedicated boss, liked to stay in headquarters. He had his apartment within the HQ set to one side away from the operations desk. The apartment had fake views of the lake and a stereo on constant replay, with the sound of the lake water lapping on the shallow banks. The natural sounds brought him closer to the outside world but he was still right there at the front line, ready for action if an emergency broke out.

As for Jamie, he preferred to stay away from the office - the farther away the better for him. He owned a humble lily pad in the centre of the silt lake. Enormous beech trees that provided just enough protection from the burning summer sun surrounded the lake.

Jamie's lily pad was one of fifty or so pads in the lake, each housing two or three frogs, so as you can imagine, it could be quite noisy at times.

At the edge of the lake there was a gaggle of Canadian geese, trained by the S.A.S., or special attack swans, the Queen's secret army. The C.G.A.F. geese fly the agents to their secret missions and carry top-secret documents back and forth from headquarters to the cabinet office in London. These geese make up the C.G.A.F. - Canadian Geese Air Force. They also ward off any would be anglers looking for a good spot to fish, so all in all they are rather good security.

Cod was talking to Jamie about a new mission when all of a sudden he stopped and swung his whole body around, creating a mini tidal wave.

"Agent J, do we have a problem keeping awake today? Have you been out calling all night or just thinking about that lovely little tree frog? What was her name?" Cod asked himself. "Ah yes, that was it, Freda." He giggled.

"Sorry, boss. I was thinking about my lily pad and," Jamie paused for a second, "nothing happens any more. Not since we stopped the mosquito pandemic."

A mosquito army had nearly wiped out an entire colony of blue-toed tree frogs in one night. The frogs had taken refuge at the silt lake after a ferocious forest fire destroyed their home. Agents Jamie Pond and Red managed to confuse the mosquitoes with stun grenades and catch the whole army of flying killing machines in a giant fishing net conveniently left behind by a forgetful angler.

"You're doing it again J," Cod continued. "We have a situation in Salisbury...."

"What's that then boss?" Jamie asked excitedly.

"If you can please be quiet and let me finish, I will enlighten you," Cod replied angrily. "Right. Something has been happening to the water voles, frogs, and newts in the area. We have already sent Agent L deep undercover, but I need you to go and relieve her, Jamie."

"But she can take care of herself Boss. She's a big girl now," Jamie demanded. *Besides, if she needs a wee she should just go and do it. She doesn't need to wait for me,* he thought, looking confused.

"No arguments J," Cod replied.

Jamie rolled his great big yellow bulbous eyes at Cod's demand and continued with his daydream. He could see himself waking up on a great big lily pad deep inside the Amazonian rainforest, with rays of the morning sun gently warming his smooth cold skin. Monkeys were chattering in the humid tropical breeze.

He felt uneasy in his daydream, as the chattering got louder and louder until ....

"**J!**" Boomed Cod for the second time that day. "**AGENT J!**"

"Sorry, Boss I'm here now. No more daydreaming, I promise," Jamie replied.

With that, Cod carried on about the mission with Red listening intently and paying the utmost of care, but again J wondered off, this time deeper than before. He had the attention span of a rather small fly.

CHAPTER 3 - AGENT LOLA & THE C.G.A.F

Lola, a little purple and yellow-speckled tree frog, waited at the water's edge of Brookes Lake in Andover, very near to the Salisbury plains. She waited patiently, listening for the chorus of frogs, crickets and mosquitoes buzzing around, but she couldn't hear anything. All was quiet but the sound of water gently kissing the base of the lake banks, and the distant echo of a woodpecker tapping the trunk of an oak tree. Tap tap tap, the woodpecker tapped out a rhythm.

Lola crept closer to the water's edge, trying to figure out what was going on. She stopped abruptly when to her horror, lying in front of her motionless and white as a sheet, was the still body of an otter. The otter looked like it had been in a furious battle with a large bird judging by the grey feathers hanging out of its mouth and the peck marks on its body.

"There's only one bird that springs to mind with feathers like this. What on earth is going on here?" she whispered.

Lola took her backpack off, grabbed her satellite phone and dialed the number for headquarters in Tilgate.

****

Ribit Ribit. Cod's phone started ringing.

Cod picked up the phone. "Ahh, we have just been talking about you Agent L."

"YEAH, YEAH, enough of the small talk. I need you to look at this."

Lola had taken a picture of the otter and emailed it via the sat phone to Cod.

"J, go and get ready. See operations. I will get as much Intel as I can," Cod ordered Jamie.

Jamie stopped Cod and waited for the image to come through. "I want to see the picture first."

"No J, like I said go to operations immediately. That's an order," Cod boomed again.

Jamie hopped up, rolled his eyes and dragged his arms behind him, walking towards another corner of headquarters and kicking the water as he went. The wall ahead of him was blank until Jamie approached it, whereby a small touchpad appeared, set within a panel in the wall that was invisible until Jamie stood in front of it. Jamie punched his agency number, 4421, into the keypad and pressed the enter key.

****

Back at the lake, Lola hadn't noticed the long dark shadow at first that blocked out the sun behind her. She shivered, then stepped back onto a long, hard scaly toe. She gasped at the menacing figure standing at least three feet over her.

"LOLA," called a familiar, terrifying voice.

Lola stood there, speechless and motionless, looking for anything that could help in the nearby reeds. She soon realised her only hope for escape was to flip back into the pond and swim for it deep down into the silt.

"Right, this is it," she whispered.

All of a sudden, there came a whoosh of air in front of her from a long grey feathery hand. This clipped her nose as she gave the biggest hardest back flip she had ever done. Grabbing for her laser as she leaped, BANG! She fired the laser off at the figure.

BANG! She fired again. Then came another whoosh and another rush of air. This came as an advantage as the force of the wind threw her further into the pond than she could have hoped for.

SPLASH.

Lola felt an excruciating pain as her tiny purple and yellow speckled body slammed into the still water.

Winded by the impact she floated, dazed. After a few moments she revived and was relieved to find herself under water with the terrifying dark figure flying off overhead. Lola swam to the edge of the pond next to the otter, crawled out, and looked down at her satellite phone.

"Blast, I've smashed my phone. I'll have to do this the old fashioned way."

She saw, in an old oak tree to the east of the lake, a couple of wood pigeons cooing to each other.

"Does my tail look big in this?" the plumpest of the two pigeons asked.

"Don't be ridiculous, we look fat in anything Nigel," Martin replied, laughing.

"Martin would you look at that. There's a frog climbing on my back."

"Nigel, it has a laser."

"What?"

"Can I help you, young lady?" asked Martin.

"I need you two to fly me back to my home," demanded Lola.

"It has a laser and it's on my back."

"Why?" asked Martin.

"It has a laser it's on my back," Nigel said for the second time.

"Oh, do shut up Nigel," Martin, exasperated, said.

Nigel composed himself and turned his head to look at Lola. He soon realised she meant no harm just by the calming smile she gave him and he started to relax.

Lola spoke up. "Look, I need to get back to Tilgate and fast…" Pausing she looked at the two pigeons who in turn looked back at her with blank faces.

"HA, HA HA HA HA HA!" Martin and Nigel nearly wet themselves laughing. "Fast, Fast, we can't fly anywhere fast. You're looking at least a day's flight getting there."

"That must be what, nearly eighty miles," Nigel said.

"I don't care, just get me there." Lola was getting a bit agitated by this time.

"You didn't say the magic word," the pigeons said in chorus.

"Magic word oh, how about I don't waste your tails with my laser. Is that magic enough?" Lola pointed her laser at Martin's snotty beak.

"Ok ok, we will take you. You will need to show us the way...and what's your name?" Nigel asked.

Lola got comfortable on Nigel's back, leant forward and whispered in his feathery ear, "Lola."

****

Back at headquarters Jamie faced the secret door, waiting for it to reveal itself.

The door creaked as it turned. *Oh my, does everything need replacing in this place? I must make a complaint to FR (Frog Resources),* he thought.

He walked into an enormous vaulted room, well enormous for Jamie, as he was about eleven inches high. However, this room was at least a couple of metres high and could if needed fit a human, under restraint of course.

Humans were banned from headquarters due to the fact that they kept stepping on frog legs and fish fins.

Jamie looked around the room, seeing gadgets and gizmos everywhere and a few testing areas. In one area, they had a dummy heron's body set up next to a dog loo and a ticking device next to it. Jamie closed his eyes and winced before... BANG! the dog loo exploded, sending the heron high up into the vaulted ceiling in a million tiny pieces, while poo rained down all over the work benches in a pungent mess.

Jamie held his nose and saw a familiar frog standing at a contraption that looked like a big blender with a rocket on both sides, and a harness attached. Agent Jack, Ph.D., head of gadgets and counter defense, had been testing out a new gadget and caught his finger in it just as he was about to let go. Jack was wearing one of those long lab coats. It was covered in burn marks and had poo splatters across the back from an earlier explosion.

"Ah, Agent J, how the devil are you old chap? Still chasing the tree frogs are you?" Jack asked in a very posh voice, despondent at his fellow agent's desire for such fanciful creatures as tree frogs.

Jack had an upbringing from a very rich country farmer. He only ate hand reared flies and had an entire large pond to himself in his owner's back garden. Until the farmer's son, Jacob, had grown up, whereupon Jacob's father decided enough was enough and the pond had to go. He wanted more space for his chickens, besides his son had left for university and had no time for such things as a pond.

Jamie, on the other hand and as Jack had stated, loved tree frogs. There is a particular place in Jamie's heart for them. His last girlfriend was a tree frog called Freda. She used to work for foreign intelligence in London. That was until a Russian pike had eaten her. She had tried to infiltrate Russian Intelligence in Moscow, but got herself detected and ended up as a rather yucky garlic dish.

Jamie hopped over to Jack, creating a lot of mess along the way from his splashing. "What have you got for me then Jack?" Jamie asked, holding his nose.

"You need to pay attention to this Agent J," Jack demanded. "This is the latest gadget I have developed."

"What is it then? Come on, you're wasting too much time," Jamie said excitedly.

"Look, calm down Agent J and let me begin."

Jack managed to calm Jamie down, and grabbed at a gadget that looked like a giant mobile phone. It was, in fact, a… well, let's allow Jack to explain.

"This, agent J, is your new communicator. It has satellite navigation, plus voice and flipper print recognition.

It can unlock any electronic keypad and delivers a bolt of 50,000 volts into any would-be assassin with the press of this button." Jack stretched his fingers around the device, reaching for the centre button on the front of it.

"WHOA watch it Jack," Jamie said, backing away.

When Jamie turned to walk away, he lifted his feet up out of the water to see if he had stepped in something. Jack stopped Jamie and gave him a backpack that was rather heavy and made Jamie groan as he put it on.

"You stink Agent Jack. What aftershave are you wearing, is it eu de dog poo?"

Agent Jack soon realised that the dog loo had smothered him in little splatters of poo from the earlier explosion. He cleared his throat and beckoned Jamie over to the exit.

"Enclosed in the backpack is your mission brief and the rest of your usual gadgets, and please read the brief when you're in flight this time Jamie."

In his pack was a set of lock picks, a code breaker, and a coil of explosive sticky stuff that looked a little like bubble gum. However, I don't think Jamie should chew it!

"On your way soldier, you can try out the new transporter I've had installed." Agent Jack patted Jamie on the back with a rather smelly hand.

Jamie walked towards the back of the research room. He raised his hand to another touchpad in the corner of the gadget room. He could still smell the poo on his shoulder. This touchpad was not so secret, it just said EXIT in big bold green letters above the pad. He placed his four smooth fingers on it. A warm glow appeared under the glass touchpad and a trap door under Jamie's feet sprung open, plunging Jamie into a dark abyss.

The fall was only a couple of feet below the trap door entrance and the landing was quite soft, but it was still hard enough to knock the wind out of him.

He sat back in the chair he had been thrown into, where two straps automatically wrapped around his body and pulled him back further into the seat. He didn't even have time to take his backpack off. The straps were now even tighter than before and pulled the gadget-filled pack into his back.

He had landed in a rocket-propelled monorail car. Jamie sat there for a few seconds when a countdown began 10 – 9 – 8 – 7 – 6; an alarm sounded at 6 - 5 – 4; Jamie panicked, 3 – 2. Jamie clutched at the sides of the monorail car so tightly his green knuckles turned white. The countdown ended and Jamie was thrust back into the seat as the monorail car launched along a long dark tunnel. Faster and faster it travelled, forcing his lips to flap around out of control. Jamie could just make out a blurry light ahead, approaching fast.

He closed his eyes just for a second but when he reopened them, he didn't even realise he had stopped. He sat there for a few more seconds panting in time with the pounding of his heart.

He shook his head and rubbed his great big yellow eyes, while a soft voice could be heard. "Please step out of the car to the right and climb the ladder to exit." The message repeated a few times as Jamie was rising out of his seat.

Jamie turned and looked at the car and said, "I am not doing that again."

Well that's what he thinks!

Jamie climbed up the ladder in front of him, awkwardly because of the backpack. The climb didn't get any easier the further he went as the passage narrowed towards the top. His shoulders chafed from the straps of his backpack as he ascended the ladder. When he reached the top another trapdoor sprang open, and Jamie squinted his eyes as he emerged from the shaft. He found himself in the middle of the C.G.A.F. mess room.

"Ah, another victim, err I mean passenger for us," a voice bellowed from the back of the mess room.

"Huh." Jamie started to look a little worried at this comment.

"Don't worry me old chum," said a more familiar voice behind him.

The voice belonged to his former academy partner Flapper, a very welcome voice after his tunnel ordeal. Flapper was a one of a kind. He was the finest of the geese in his squadron. His feathers were in pristine condition and always shone as he took very good care of himself.

The other geese in the mess room all turned away from Jamie and went back to their milkshakes when Flapper walked over to him.

"Come on Jamie, you're flying with me today mate," Flapper exclaimed in his deep Canadian accent.

"Ok, but only 'cause it's you," Jamie answered.

Jamie stopped and looked at Flapper who in turn smirked as ten pairs of goose eyes glared at him after his comment. The other geese didn't take kindly to this. Jamie's pace quickened slightly with nervousness when he left the mess room. Flapper sniggered as they walked.

Jamie stopped on the jetty outside of the mess room and took a deep breath. It felt cool and calming. He checked his shorts and buttoned up the top button of his khaki safari shirt. He thought to himself that he should have put his body warmer on ready for the flight.

"Oh well, too late now," he whispered under his breath as he prepared to climb onto Flapper's back.

Flapper jumped into the still water, extended his left wing out, and asked Jamie to climb on his back.

There was a harness on Flapper's back looking empty, waiting for someone to fill its worn webbing straps. Jamie climbed up, strapped himself in and patted Flapper on the back.

Flapper turned his long neck around. "All set mate?"

Jamie didn't answer, and just gave a look of despair to Flapper.

"Oh Ok. Let's go then," Flapper said to Jamie.

Flapper turned back his long neck to face forward and look up at air traffic control in front but just to the side of them. He extended his right wing and gave a salute.

The air traffic control was, in fact, two woodpeckers that checked the lake for any obstacles before allowing any geese to take off.

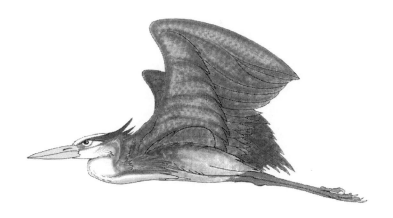

CHAPTER 4 - FLUFFY BEAR

In a dark log cabin in Salisbury just south of Porton Down, a sinister laugh echoed across the plains.

"What's the matter boss? You're laughing for no apparent reason," asked one of the Heron's henchmen.

"Silence, infidel you know nothing… I was just thinking about my devious plan," Heron replied and laughed aloud again.

"What would that be? Let us guess um World domination or no…. I know. You're going to wipe out all the animals in Salisbury, gas all the humans and then steal…"

"Ok, ok stop it. Did you read my diary again Snatch?" Heron asked.

"No, you copied everyone into the email you wrote to your mother telling her about your latest plan. Fluffy bear, is that what she calls you?" Snatch asked.

"WHAT?" Heron was a bit embarrassed at Snatch's discovery.

"That's what you put at the end of the email." Snatch sniggered again.

"QUIET!" The Heron shouted. "That's enough! I'm not paying you to sit here and mock me. Find me the entrance to the underground weapons area and get me the human scientist I asked you for."

"Pay us. When was the last time you paid us then?" a few of the disgruntled henchmen piped up.

After The Heron's comment about pay, there was a loud flap of wings and black feathers flying everywhere. Snatch, next to The Heron, waited patiently to receive his special orders.

"Snatch, go and talk to your buddy Hacker the Hawk. If I am correct, that awful Jamie Pond should be in flight about now heading towards Lola. Ask him to find out what J is doing and then leave him there. I don't want him harmed yet! I have a bigger plan for him."

"Can't we just stretch him a little?" Snatch asked.

"No! Not yet, I want to be there to watch his demise on the plains when he finally arrives." Heron laughed that sinister laugh again.

Snatch was the Heron's right-hand man. He belonged to the most despicable race of creatures - the sewer rat. He has never wanted to be anything else. As a henchman, his most useful trait was the ability to gain access to anywhere undetected and pick any lock known to human and vermin. There wasn't a safe in the world that he couldn't open. He also had a thing for stretching his victims and then scratching them very slowly to get information from them. It generally worked very well, which is why The Heron said not yet.

D.P. Hall

CHAPTER 5 - THE ARROW OF DOOM

Jamie scanned the horizon as they flew over skyscrapers, long rolling hills and small villages. They had been in flight for about forty minutes when Flapper noticed two of the largest wood pigeons he had ever seen headed straight for them.

"Hold on, this is going to get bumpy," Flapper shouted to warn Jamie of the impending collision.

Jamie locked his arms tight into Flappers harness and dug his heels into the stirrups. Flapper banked left then right, up left again then nose-dived to avoid a collision, but the pigeons kept coming. Jamie opened his eyes for a second and saw what looked like Lola waving her arms frantically and pointing towards the cluttered rooftops of Winchester town centre. Jamie gestured back with thumbs up.

"Flapper, land on top of one of those buildings. Lola wants to meet up," Jamie shouted above the noise of Flappers beating wings.

"Aye aye, Skipper," Flapper replied.

When Jamie and Lola landed amongst rooftop aerials and satellite dishes, Jamie unclipped the harness before he grabbed his backpack and rested it in his seat. He then jumped to one side straight into the middle of a pile of stacked up straw.

"My goodness, this is a crow's nest. Of all the places to land you touched down next to one."

"You said pick a roof, Jamie," Flapper replied.

Crows do not like frogs except as food. They have a tendency to serve them up as a garlic dish for their mothers on Sundays.

Lola arrived.

"We haven't got long," Jamie said.

"No I can see that from the straw you're standing in," Lola replied.

"What happened? Why didn't you wait for me?" asked Jamie.

"Somebody unexpected showed up and he nearly got the better of me," said Lola.

"Who...Who was it?" Jamie stammered nervously. He had a sudden feeling of impending doom as he thought he already knew what Lola was going to say.

Then she said it.

"THE HERON."

****

Back at headquarters, Red was working on some security updates with Director Cod when an alarm startled him. It was very loud, even from underwater.

Cod looked at Red and under his breath said, "Rookie."

A giant TV screen emerged from the water near where Cod and Red were standing. It stood almost three feet high, which is quite tall when you are only eleven inches tall yourself.

"COD," a voice boomed from the rather large speakers, causing ripples in the water around them. "I need you to send agent J to parliament to protect the deputy prime minister when he addresses the commons. What he will have to say is going to upset a lot of people." It was the Secretary of Defence giving the order.

Nervously Cod answered, "But Secretary, I have already sent J elsewhere on other matters of national security."

"I could do it boss, because J has taught me everything he knows. What do you think? Please send me in there." Red waited nervously for an answer.

"WHAT?" The Secretary boomed again. "No offence Red, but I don't want some rookie taking J's place. There is a lot riding on this as you well know Director Cod," the Secretary of Defence added.

"Look, I can do this. I'm superb at counter surveillance boss," Red piped up.

"It's not that. Red you are limited to where you can go, as you're a fish! Why do you think I am stuck here at headquarters? Besides I have big plans for you here," Cod explained to Red.

Cod was getting old. He was nearly sixty, which for a carp is amazing as they generally only live to be around fifty years of age. He was looking for a replacement to take over the operations at the C.F.I.A. headquarters.

Cod had been keeping a watchful eye on Red and thought he had great potential, enough to fill the most prestigious position of the Director of Intelligence, but hey that's another story. Back to our heroes on the rooftops.

****

Jamie was startled when Lola said the Heron's name.

"What happened then? Did he try to capture you or did he...?" Jamie said nervously.

"Jamie calm down. I was investigating the disappearance of all the pond dwellers in Salisbury when it went dark all of a sudden, and there he was as tall and menacing as he could be! It terrified me Jamie. I thought he was going to finish me off," Lola explained.

Both Jamie and Lola stopped in silence. In the distance, Lola could hear the faint sound of impending doom. The crows were coming.

Jamie stared into space, still thrown by what Lola had just told him. He didn't notice Lola prodding him and shouting, "JAMIE, COME ON."

Then Jamie saw it. The black shadows in an arrow-shaped formation swooping in with such force that the clouds around them were parting like curtains blowing open in the wind.

You see, no one had listened to The Heron when he asked them to leave J until he reached the Plains at Salisbury.

Jamie jumped into action. "Sorry Lola, let's go."

They both climbed on the back of Flapper and strapped themselves in. Before they could say they were ready, Flapper leapt into the air, beating his wings ferociously and blowing crows nests everywhere, trying to get as much lift off as he could muster.

Lola shouted back at the pigeons, "Thank you for the lift guys, and sorry about the mess on your back."

"What mess on my back? Yuck is that...." Nigel cringed at the thought of what could have been wee on his back, but it was juice that Lola had spilt from her drink bottle.

The intrepid spies looked back at the pigeons. Just above they could see the arrowhead of doom turn from the rooftop and head straight towards them.

Flapper turned his long neck back to Jamie and Lola, before looking up at the crows swooping in for an attack. "Hold on you two, this is going to get a bit hairy."

Flapper dipped his left wing and descended into a spiral, searching for a warm thermal to try to get a powerful lift. He found that thermal, and Jamie and Lola were thrown back with immense force as Flapper's speed increased tenfold, rising up higher and higher above the clouds. Jamie strained his body to look back for the crows but saw nothing but clouds and blue sky around them.

"Well, looks like you pulled it off Flapper! Well done me old mate," Jamie said, patting Flappers long sleek neck.

"Jamie, don't count your chickens yet, look below us."

Jamie leaned over the side of Flapper with the wind beating against the side of his face, and saw through the cloud breaks the dark arrow of doom rising ever closer through the clouds.

Jamie turned to Lola. "Brace yourself, this is going to be a bumpy ride again Lola."

With that, Flapper drew his head back, raised his tail and tilted his wings forward, and then he performed a nail-biting nosedive.

The force of the dive was so intense Jamie could see the whites of his knuckles as he clung on to the harness for dear life.

Suddenly Lola shouted at Jamie, " HELP ME JAMIE!"

She was starting to lose her grip of the harness.

"TAKE MY HAND LOLA!" Jamie reached out a smooth green hand to grab at Lola but was already too late.

Lola had lost her hold and was flailing out of control with only a cord from her belt attached to Flapper's harness, spinning over and over. Jamie grabbed once again and caught the cord, and just in time. The cord had snapped at Flappers end.

Jamie pulled Lola into his chest. "Got you."

Lola sighed, for a moment she felt safe in Jamie's arms.

Flapper's dive had become more intense as he rocketed through the clouds like a heat-seeking missile. Flapper could see through the clearing clouds the crows in front of him turning up towards them. He adjusted his direction slightly and shot past the crows like a bullet cutting through a sea of feathers.

The crows tried to turn to face our heroes, but as they did a couple lost control and crashed into one, then another and then another, making the rabble plummet to the ground at a hundred miles an hour. Closer and closer they tumbled until thump! The crows slammed into the ground. All you could see was a cloud of dust and black feathers floating gently back to the ground.

Jamie stretched his head over the side of Flapper again as the bird finally began to slow down to a gentle glide, spiraling in a circle above the feathery mess.

"Lola, look at that. They came they tried, they crashed and burned baby."

"Yes, Jamie, and don't call me baby."

"Let's go kids. We need to get back and report to Cod," Flapper said.

CHAPTER 6 - FLIGHT OF THE BALD EAGLES

Meanwhile, back in the deep wooded area behind Salisbury plains, a dark plot was thickening.

An even darker figure was standing above his minions. "Ladies and gentlemen, the day we strike back against the once great army C.F.I.A. is nearly upon us."

A tremendous cheer from the gathering of dark assassins erupted as The Heron began his speech.

"We will not be suppressed anymore! We will become victorious and drive out this scourge of do-gooders for the last time. The time of the bird has arrived. No one will dare challenge us when our brothers from afar join us in two days, and then the attack will begin."

Whispering among the assassins spread like wildfire over a dry heath land.

"Who will be joining us, Heron?" asked his trusty rat at arms.

"Why! The bald eagles are coming, dear boy," Heron answered.

Snatch gulped and looked at the others, then back at Heron. "They're savage, Heron. Do we have to bring them in on this? They are more likely to take over rather than help. Do you remember the last time we asked for their help?"

"How could I forget, but we need a little more air support when we go into the bunkers and take the weapon," Heron replied.

The humans had developed a powerful weapon that had the power to send a whole army or city into another dimension. It used sound waves from large quartz crystals to alter physical particles from cryonic fusion. The weapon would open a hole in the very fabric of space and time, transporting everything in the blast radius to another dimension. The humans called it the Ripper. They had decided it was too powerful to use and buried it deep in an old military research bunker hidden in plain sight at a secret M.O.D. (Ministry of Defense) research base at Porton Down.

Amongst the cheering crowd, a dark figure was pushing its way through, knocking magpies and sparrowhawks over like bowling pins.

"Heron, look! Here comes Shifty, and he looks like he's had a bit of bother." Snatch grabbed at Herons feathery wing as he said this.

"Get off me Snatch, I can see!"

Shifty was a starling and very good at being Heron's top spy, but this day he seemed a bit worse for wear. "Heron I. I. I have to tell you something," Shifty blurted at Heron.

"Calm down Shifty, catch your breath. What's the problem?" Heron looked a bit worried at this point as Shifty only ever came to see him if there was imminent danger.

"The crows, they.....they are all gone, sir. Jamie and Lola escaped them and caused the crows to crash into the ground. I saw the whole thing. My good gosh that goose can fly."

"What are you talking about Shifty? They were my best attack squadron. Who ordered the attack? I thought I said wait until Jamie is on the Plains before we attack him."

"Yes who ordered the attack?" Snatch added, scowling at the baying flock. He knew he had ordered the crows to attack, going against the Heron's orders.

The Heron stopped talking because in the distance he heard the terrifying cry of their American brothers.

"Who turned off the lights?" Snatch asked nervously.

"That's not the lights Snatch. Look at them, they're beautiful...but so deadly," Heron replied

"And early," added Shifty.

All you could see for miles was the beating of rather large wings from the bloodthirsty bald eagles. The sun was blotted out like an eclipse. There was a beam of light now and then when eagle wings lifted and lowered.

The Heron was startled by a loud thud and looked around. Behind him and standing at head height with him was a rather war torn looking bird covered in scars from old battles.

"Howdy Heron. What have you been doing with the empire since I have been away?" asked the commanding chief of the bald eagles in his thick southern accent.

"Ahh, Frank you're early. How are you brother?" Heron and Frank went back a long way.

Frank had helped the Heron in the past until he had been sent word that his family back home in Alaska was having trouble with a rival gang of buzzards. That was the last The Heron had seen of Frank until now. Snatch was pleased with this. Frank was always getting in the way and every time he looked at Snatch, well, Snatch felt like he was about to become Frank's lunch.

"Enough of the niceties Heron, let's get down to business. From this moment, where do we stand with your operation?" asked Frank.

"Well, my American friend! We are a day away from taking the weapon, and if Agent J would just give up we are close to gaining control of C.F.I.A. as well," answered Heron.

As soon as the Heron mentioned Jamie's name the eagles started whispering and murmuring amongst themselves. There was a sudden whoosh like a tornado as the bald eagles fled from the forest. Feathers and fallen leaves went flying into the air. The force was so powerful that it knocked over the ravens and magpies that were waiting patiently for their orders.

When the feathers and leaves gently cascaded back down to the earth, The Heron shouted at Frank, "Where are they going? I don't believe this. Jamie is a frog, why does everyone run away when I mention his name?"

"Look Heron, he almost single handedly destroyed the mosquito armies. If he was just a frog how did he do that? He really is a force to be reckoned with," Frank explained.

"Now there are only five of you."

"Oh, relax Heron. The others are only here because they didn't hear you say the J word." Frank added, "I shouldn't mention it, or we may lose them as well."

Heron and Frank sat down and discussed the coming events whilst the now small army of magpies and ravens prepared for dinner.

****

Jamie leaned over to Lola after landing safely back at Tilgate silt lake, "That was a close shave Lola, we wouldn't have made it that time if hadn't have been for Flapper's awesome flying!"

"Yes Jamie, let's get in to see Cod and tell him about our findings," said Lola.

This time they went in through the back door. The door was hidden in the undergrowth at the back of the lake. Again there was a touchpad shaped like a frog's hand. This one also had a voice recognition port. Jamie said his name into the port and put his hand on the pad. A soft whirring noise could be heard over the croaking of other frogs in the lake.

"Here we go Lola," Jamie said.

"I'm sorry, please repeat!" a mechanical voice interrupted Jamie.

"Oh come on...." Jamie paused.

"*Voice print recognized.*"

With that, the floor beneath their feet opened and in dropped Lola and Jamie.

Flapper headed back to the C.G.A.F. after both agents had disappeared through the floor. The fall caught Jamie by surprise as it did every time he went in through the back door of the C.F.I.A. but not Lola. Cool as a cucumber she landed on to her two webbed feet. She looked into Jamie's eyes, and then shook her head as he picked himself up. The trap door above them closed shut with a clunk when the locks slid into place.

"Jamie do hurry up, we need to report to Cod," Lola explained.

"Alright Lola, don't get your knickers in a twist."

Lola turned away from Jamie and headed into the dark passage. The darkness was soon driven back by bright lights as one by one the lights flickered into life, revealing the same car Jamie had ridden on earlier that morning. Nervously Jamie side stepped around it to the other side and following Lola into the car sat down.

"Do we have to do this? I don't like this at all, Lola."

After the morning's trip, Jamie didn't want to go anywhere near this car, ever!

Lola could see the tension in Jamie's eyes so she extended her smooth purple hand and held his, just as the car's seat belt wrapped around them and they rocketed off into the tunnel.

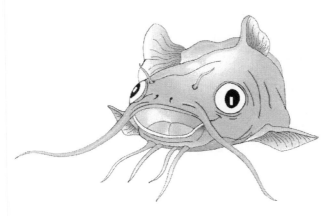

CHAPTER 7 - SPECIAL AGENT RED

"Ah, there you are Agents J and L, and not before time. No time to settle in, I need your report on today's events," Cod said.

Cod beckoned Jamie and Lola over to his office, using his rather old war torn fin.

"Shall I begin Sir?" Lola asked cod.

Lola began to tell of her encounter with The Heron at the small lake and her daring escape. She also mentioned meeting Jamie on the rooftops and being chased by the kamikaze crows.

Jamie stood up and added, "The Heron has risen again. We know this much now, and he is planning something big."

"Hmm, you could be right there, Agent J," Cod replied. "Yes and I think he is gathering his flocks as we speak."

Jamie added again, "When we were flying away from the crows I could see a dark shadow in the distance. It looked to be coming from the Atlantic."

"Where is The Heron hiding now? What of this shadow? These are the questions and I need to know the answers so I can report to the Defense Secretary, Agents J and L." Cod was looking very anxious as he asked the questions.

"What's the matter Sir?" asked Lola.

Cod raised his large brown head at Lola, and she knew what the matter was deep down in her heart but didn't want to say anything in front of Jamie. Cod was getting old. Lola could see that in him and felt his sorrow. She knew someone else would take his place, and Cod would be placed in some secret location (probably Bognor Regis). Brainwashed of all the secret information he had access to as the chief of operations, and he and his family given a new identity. You see, once a spy always a spy. Jamie turned his body quickly in the swivel chair he was sitting in, only to see his best friend and partner Red standing over him, dressed in a shirt and tie. Red had little round rimmed glasses on the end of his spiky nose.

Jamie sniggered. "Is there a fancy dress party?"

"Ha, Ha hilarious Agent J," said Red.

Cod piped up at this point to save any more embarrassment on Jamie's part. "Agent J, meet my new assistant director, Special Agent R."

"You have got to be kidding me," Jamie protested.

"Look J, he has all the makings of a great leader," Cod replied.

"Red, we need to talk," said Jamie.

"Not now, and you should be calling me Sir," Red explained.

"There are more pressing things to be dealing with."

Jamie turned his chair back to Cod and shook his head, Cod put up his withered fin and said, "Agent J, go back to Salisbury and find out what you can." Cod looked at Lola. " Go with him Lola, back him up and report your findings directly to special agent Red. Take Flapper and be as quick as you can. I expect your report in this evening."

"If we are not too late by then," said Lola.

Jamie looked at Lola, then back at Red and muttered something under his breath. He stood up and walked out of the office, turning his head away from Red as he went.

"He's supposed to be my best friend. Why didn't he tell me? Oh well, this changes everything now," he muttered.

Red smiled at Lola and went on with his business with Cod.

"We have a lot to prepare, Red. I have my meeting with the defense secretary in one hour. Are my files ready?"

"Yes, boss."

Lola hurried after Jamie. "Jamie, Red's been given an excellent opportunity. You should be proud of your best mate. You're a field man and always will be, would you want to be stuck in that office twenty-four seven?"

Jamie looked at Lola and replied, "He's supposed to be my best friend. We don't have secrets from each other, you know we're supposed to stick together."

"You would have done the same, Jamie."

"You should be proud Jamie. Proud of what your friend has achieved."

"I am Lola, too proud, that's the thing."

"Come on let's go. Let's go and get that evil Heron once and for all!"

CHAPTER 8 - THE BUNKER

Hidden at the centre of Porton Down, two soldiers were on guard near the entrance of a secret bunker. They were armed to the teeth, with large machine guns and enough bullets to sink a battleship.

They were sporting rather heavy ammunition belts, which chafed around their shoulders when they moved. Being stealthy wasn't their objective. Smashing everything and anything that they didn't recognise, or were threatened by was the key to their duty at the bunker.

Bob, the taller of the two, had his head down looking over a newspaper crossword. "Seven down, a long legged bird with grey feathers and a long sharp beak, five letters?"

"I know this, it's a... HERON," Ben shouted out.

"There's no need to shout Ben."

"No Bob, look."

Bob looked up from his crossword but before he could react or duck, The Heron was upon him, knocking him unconscious to the ground. Ben backed away from The Heron, shaking as he pointed his machine gun at him.

Ben's weapon shook violently in his arms when he stumbled backwards and fired one shot off, accidentally hitting one of the circling ravens in the bottom.

The raven gave out an almighty shriek and plummeted to the ground.

Ben looked up from his fallen position and saw the raven falling towards him. Just as he tried to get up, two of the bald eagles jumped out from their hiding place and grabbed him, holding him there for the raven to have a soft landing.

Thud, the raven hit Ben straight in the stomach. He gave out a groan and saw The Heron standing over his trembling body, looking rather menacing.

The Heron leaned his long slender neck down and whispered into the guard's ear, "Hello there Mister."

The guard took one look at the Heron and was puzzled, even startled by what he had just heard. He pushed the two eagles aside and jumped up like a jack in the box. He ran as fast as his combat clad legs could carry him, screaming like a girl.

"Come on, we don't have much time," The Heron said to his assault team. "Frank, you pick the lock. Shifty, keep an eye out for any trouble," Heron added.

"OK," Frank and Shifty said in unison.

"Eagles, go and stop that guard," The Heron added.

Frank extended one of his long talons into the steel lock and began to pick it.

The Heron was becoming very nervous waiting for Frank. "Come on, this is taking too long."

The bunker was at the centre of an MOD firing range within Porton Down. One side of the entrance had a large grassy mound of earth placed over it, which the humans left to grow out of control as it gave more cover from the air. Nevertheless, the Heron knew it was there. His inside sources knew exactly where it was. They also knew what the bunker was and why the humans kept a constant guard in front of it.

As Frank turned the locks mechanism, Shifty thought he heard something in the thickest part of the surrounding forest, "Wait, shush. I can hear something," Shifty warned the others.

However, no one could hear him as the adrenaline was kicking in, when the lock Frank was picking went clunk, like a hammer striking cold steel.

The big heavy iron door sprang into action, swinging into the dark passage of the bunker.

The Heron jumped up from his crouched position and shoved Frank to one side, "Out of my way, Frank," he growled as he pushed.

Shifty piped up again. " I'm telling you guys, there is something in the forest."

Frank looked up at Shifty with a puzzled face and then looked back at the forest edge, waiting, listening. Suddenly Shifty slipped off his perch above the bunker entrance, startling Frank.

Frank stretched his wings out and with one almighty flap burst up into the air, grabbing Shifty, with his talons stopping him from falling onto the hard concrete ground around the entrance to the bunker. They both turned and headed into the dark passage, following The Heron.

"Wait for us," Frank squawked.

Walking through the dark passageways of the bunker our villains had forgotten about the noises in the forest and focused on the job at hand, locating the Ripper.

Ravens were still circling above the bunker, watching for the guard's return or worse, Agent Jamie Pond. The ravens stopped and floated effortlessly against the fresh breeze when they saw a lone guard dog emerging from the forest and head towards the bunkers entrance.

The ravens settled above the entrance and watched as the dog sat down midway between the bunker and the forest. The dog had had a tip off that something was happening in the plains. The tip off had come from the same insiders that the Heron was using.

The ravens looked at each other then looked back. "What is he doing?"

"I don't know George."

The dog turned his head back at the forest from his sitting position, barked, and then snapped his head back to the bunker.

Confused, the ravens crept backwards, never taking their eyes off the dog. They stopped suddenly as eight more vicious, drooling Rottweiler's emerged from the forest, joining the lone Rottweiler.

The humans had ordered the C.F.I.A. to fit the dogs with tracking devices and thermal imaging cameras on their collars for night operations. They also had panic buttons attached to their tails in case of life or death situations.

These gadgets had been supplied and installed by the tech guys at the C.F.I.A.

After the dogs had received their tip off they made their way from a routine patrol towards the bunker. When they approached they heard the guard called Ben screaming like a girl, and Frank picking the lock.

The two ravens ducked and slid down the grassy bunker's side protection.

"Quick, get in here," George whispered.

The ravens slipped into the bunker and flew towards The Heron and others.

CHAPTER 9 - THE RIPPER

Jamie glanced over his shoulder at Lola's windswept face, smiled, turned his head back towards Flapper and shouted, "How much longer?"

Flapper raised his head and replied, "Twenty minutes J."

"Lola, when we arrive keep your head down. I've heard the eagles are there helping The Heron."

"Don't worry Jamie. I sent a message to the canine division that something might be happening in the plains. Apparently, another agent within the Salisbury Base backed up my message. I told them to take care of the hired help," Lola reassured Jamie.

Lola was just about the only female frog he would ever listen to, apart from his mother of course.

Jamie stared up at the clouds slowly passing by, listening to Flapper's gently beating wings.

 He tried to make familiar shapes from the clouds. One looked a bit round and chubby and he immediately thought of Cod. Another was shaped like a lily pad and another resembled an old friend turned pro, Red.

****

Below the cloud line, marching across the plains, the Rottweiler guard advanced closer to the bunker. Four of the dogs waited outside the door in staggered formation as the others crept inside. The dogs turned on their thermal imaging cameras. A visor flipped over each of their heads and gave them a heads up night vision display.

The bunker was buried below the plains surface deep in the bedrock. No communicators would work under there, not even short wave radios. It was a complete radio dead zone.

The Heron walked deeper and deeper down into the bunker, setting off the security lights as he went. The lights were blinding and made The Heron squint at every turn. When the lights hit the opposite wall, it glistened with the salty residue from the seeping bedrock. The Heron walked for about another twenty yards when he saw it, the thing he was striving for. The very thing that would possibly bring an end to humankind and his biggest foe, the C.F.I.A.

In front of him were the words etched in a large steel door: DANGER. KEEP OUT. AUTHORISED PERSONNEL ONLY.

Under these words were a set of human fingerprint scanners that would unlock the door.

Judging by the thickness of the door that sealed the room behind, there was no way he would gain access by simply blowing it off its hinges with explosives. *How on earth am I going to get in there,* he thought.

As the Heron pondered on his predicament, Frank came bounding down the passage, bumping into the Heron and nearly knocking him to the ground.

"Ah, you brought Shifty with you. We need his skills here right now!" Heron boomed at Frank and Shifty rather excitedly.

"Good job I did come down with you then Heron wasn't it?" Frank boomed back.

The Heron looked at Shifty.

"I know. You need me to access the fingerprint scanner."

"Well, how about that. There is a brain in there," The Heron replied to Shifty's comment.

As Shifty tapped numbered keys on the drop down keypad under the first fingerprint scanner, the army of dogs crept ever closer through the tunnel, switching off the light sensors as they went.

The Heron looked over at Shifty and snarled like a rabid dog. "Come on Shifty, we need to get in there. The Ripper is waiting for me, I can almost see it," Heron boomed again.

Heron's boom could not have come at a worse time for him. The echo of his booming voice alerted the dogs outside of the bunker and gave them a sense of urgency.

"Come on, that's the Heron," the lead Rottweiler whispered to the others.

Shifty punched in a few more number combinations when suddenly a bead of light flooded the surrounding tunnel. The Heron, Shifty, and Frank squeezed their eyes shut, blocking the blinding light. It became stronger as the door opened wider, revealing a platform and a cat ladder that descended into a massive chamber.

Just next to the platform there was a caged goods lift with a decal saying: NO PASSENGERS.

The Heron slowly removed his wing from his eyes and pushed the other two to one side. "Let me through," he said forcefully.

Heron hopped into the goods lift and pressed the down button. The lift hadn't been used for a long while and creaked as it whirred into motion.

The chamber was about seventy feet in height, and that again in width and length. Lime had seeped through the walls leaving white streaked stains on the concrete and small salty stalactites hanging from the ceiling.

It looked like someone had drawn the streaks onto the walls using a lump of enormous chalk. He looked around the room, noticing the hundreds of rows of jars filled with a brown murky liquid and...

"Oh, my that's a raven in that jar." He paused and looked again. "What have the humans been up to now?" The Heron whispered to no one but himself.

The others joined him, awaiting Heron's instructions.

"What are we looking for, Heron?" Frank asked rather impatiently.

"Look, my feathery friend. There should be a large rounded plastic box with a radioactive sign imprinted on it and a keypad with the words, The Ripper, written on the side of it," Heron answered.

Now you would have thought the humans would have written something less conspicuous on the box. However, no, there it was lying on a bloodstained steel operating table, the word RIPPER in big bold yellow letters on the side of the box.

"Ahh, there it is," Heron sniggered as he walked towards the table.

"It's mine. I have found it! Now we can bring an end to all things C.F.I.A." The Heron seemed very pleased with himself as he said these words.

Shifty and Frank looked at each other and gulped, "He has. I told you, he's gone nuts."

Heron opened the box, which of course, the humans hadn't locked. The cover creaked as he lifted it.

Heron groaned at the weight of the lid and let it slam onto the table, causing an almighty echo through the chamber and up through the tunnels. The Heron took the Ripper out of the box. It was conveniently handheld and very light. The weapon even had a soft user-friendly gel-filled grip. He pointed it towards Shifty and Frank.

"Whoa, what are you doing Heron? Put that thing down. You're likely to hurt someone or even worse, us," Frank ordered The Heron.

Nevertheless, The Heron didn't listen to Frank and grasped the arming mechanism with his feathery hand. It slid back into place with a clunk.

Frank had a sudden moment of panic and started jabbering at the Heron. "Look Heron, put it…. HERON…. Put…. HERON just stop, don't…."

Just then, the angry pack of dogs burst through the chamber door, falling over each other as they tumbled into the doorway.

The kerfuffle ended suddenly. The dogs had just enough time to glance down and see The Heron pointing the Ripper at them, and then a blinding light engulfed the dogs, suffocating them in its brightness. The light lasted for a few seconds but quickly receded back to the dimly lit emergency lights of the chamber.

Frank spun around and gasped, "Where, what the? Where did they go?" Puzzled, Frank turned back to the Heron, who was wearing a sly evil villain grin.

"See the power the humans have stumbled across!" Heron snarled at Frank and Shifty.

"This is what we will use to destroy the C.F.I.A.," Heron snarled again. "Now you two come here and grab the case. I will carry the Ripper," Heron demanded.

CHAPTER 10 - FUNNY VOICES

Jamie, Lola, and Flapper finally reached the plains after a long four-hour flight. During their flight they had seen a strange blinding beam of light shooting past them like a rocket launching into out of space. A deafening clap of thunder followed closely after the beam had shot by. Flapper's right wing had just skimmed the light beam without him realising as they flew past it, and some of his feathers had disappeared. Flapper hadn't realised because of the blinding light.

Jamie's vision came back, blurry at first, but clearing after a few seconds. "What in the blazes was that Flapper?"

"I don't know, but my wing hurts, it's like something is missing," Flapper replied.

Lola shook her head at their conversation whilst looking down at the plains, scouring the area for the Heron and his hordes of bald eagles. She couldn't see anything down there, only a few humans running around like headless chickens.

"Flapper, your wing is smoking," Jamie alerted Flapper to the smoldering mess of feathers on his right wing.

"Oh…Oh my goodness." Flapper started to panic and slipped into a nosedive without any form of control at all.

"Uh oh, here we go again. Lola, hang on," Jamie shouted.

The soldiers who were investigating the noise and alleged encounters with talking birds all stopped, and raised their heads towards the sky.

Flapper raced towards them at such a speed he was creating a vortex through every cloud break. The soldiers ran in all directions, this way and that, bumping into each other. Finally, after a few bruised heads and chipped teeth they fell on top of each of other, making a soldier mountain.

Lola shook her head again at the pile of soldiers and thought, *I like doing this job, but no wonder the world's security is always in peril. The humans have no idea of self control at all.* Lola didn't hold a lot of respect for humans. They kept her pond clear of weeds and provided lots of rubbish for the flies to lay their eggs on, everything else just didn't really matter.

Flapper managed to gather enough strength from his undamaged wing to bring them out of the nosedive just in time, saving them from a messy end on the hard, dry plains surface. He landed right on top of the bunkers entrance.

Jamie and Lola unclipped their harnesses and jumped in unison off Flapper's back straight on to a pile of bird poo.

Jamie yelped, looking down at his rather messy foot while Lola sniggered at his misfortune. "That's supposed to be lucky you know J," Lola chortled.

"Yeah, lucky for whom though? You didn't step in bird poo," Jamie snarled at Lola.

With that, Lola turned, walking away from Jamie and heading for the half open bunker door when all of a sudden she disappeared from Jamie's line of sight.

Jamie looked down at Lola and started laughing. "Ha Ha, who's laughing now Lola. At least I'm not wearing bird poo as my coat."

Lola had slipped over in the same pile of poo Jamie had stepped in. *Ugh, that's going to stink,* she thought. Saying nothing she stood up from the poo, looked at Flapper and totally blanked Jamie. She proceeded from the messy situation towards the tunnel entrance, trying to brush off the poo as she went. Jamie sniggered in the background as she did so.

"Oh do shut up J," Lola scolded Jamie.

The intrepid trio ventured deep down into the dark tunnels of the bunker, cautiously trying not to disturb any would-be attackers. The tunnel felt eerily quiet. Water gently trickled through the decrepit concrete walls, which glistened from the warm yellow glow of the security lights. The water in some places had formed a green algae barrier on the walls that almost made Jamie feel nostalgic for his lily pad.

"What is that smell?" Lola said holding her nose.

The stench grew stronger the deeper they ventured into the bunker.

Flapper grabbed Lola's arm. "It smells of wet dog, Lola."

Lola agreed with Flapper. "Can you two hear something?" she asked Flapper and Jamie.

Lola thought she could hear faint barking coming from up ahead but shook her head, thinking, *No it can't be. There would have been guard dogs outside when we came in.*

Jamie wasn't looking where he was going and stumbled over a raised floor grate, hitting his smooth green speckled chin on the cold steel grated floor, causing a small graze. He picked himself up, rubbing his chin and nursing his wound. His eyes grew wide when he saw cold burn marks on the walls around them and chunks of dog fur frozen into the burn marks.

"What on earth happened here?" he said to the others.

Lola had already started to examine the damage to the chambers entrance. Flapper spread his impressive wings and glided down to the chamber floor. He was looking for any clues to what had happened and why The Heron had chosen to raid this bunker in particular. Flapper scanned over the metal workbenches but saw nothing of any significance, apart from a clean spot on a steel operating table at the centre of the chamber.

Lola finished examining the burn marks, saw Jamie nursing his chin and asked, "Ahh Jamie are you, ok love, you seem to have a little blood on your chin."

"Yes thank you, Lola. Never mind me, what have you got there?" Jamie replied.

"It's almost as if there used to be something living here, but not? Still here, still in this place but not," Lola answered.

Jamie looked at Lola. "Lola you have evidently gone quite mad. I'm calling Red, he can have you looked at later."

Little did Lola know how close to the truth she was. Lola and Jamie descended into the chamber and joined Flapper at the centre table.

Flapper was reading a document with the words: "TOP SECRET". Official instruction manual for the Ripper.'

"That's what the Heron has taken, and I fear used against the dogs in that doorway," Lola blurted out.

"Yeah, but what is it Lola?" Jamie asked.

"The Ripper temporal displacement field generator. When activated the Ripper will generate a displacement in the very fabric of space and time. The displacement causes items in the blast zone to fall into a deep sleep and then force the victims through the temporal rip, sending them to another dimension or time," Flapper piped up, reading the document.

There were also the words printed diagonally across each page: DECOMMISSIONED. DANGEROUS. DO NOT USE. NOT TESTED.

"Ok Flapper. A simple time vortex gun would have done!" Jamie tutted at Flapper.

"Seems like it has been used, and was tested now doesn't it?" Lola looked up at the chamber entrance as she spoke and shook her head again.

"Do you think The Heron used it on the dog squad then Lola?" Jamie looked horrified, but also disbelieving as Lola acknowledged his question with a firm nod of her head.

Flapper walked across the room looking for more clues as to what had happened in the chamber, other than the obvious.

There were locked wooden boxes containing secret documents and other boxes containing nothing, well it looked like nothing through the glass access panels on the side of the boxes, until you moved a little closer that is. Then suddenly, BANG! crashing against the glass was a creature looking back at you with crazy yellow eyes and oozing what looked like snot from the corners of its mouth. Flapper jumped back from the crazy eyed creature then jumped again when he bumped into Jamie.

"Oh, sorry J, didn't see you there."

Jamie just rolled his eyes at Flapper and carried on with his investigation.

"J, Flapper, have you two finished clowning around? We need to get after Heron before he uses the Ripper again on some poor unsuspecting pond life," Lola shouted but with no avail.

Flapper and Jamie had found a voice changer in one of the boxes and were using it on each other.

"I WILL CHANGE MY VOICE YOU WILL BE EATEN IF YOU DO NOT COMPLY." Jamie had the first go, it made his voice all shaky like he was sitting on a pneumatic drill.

"Oh, that's funny J. Can we just get moving?" Lola demanded again.

"Hey, it's my turn, J." Flapper snatched the voice changer from Jamie's smooth green hand.

"YOU WILL CLEAN MY TOILET OR I WILL SNOT ON YOU." Flapper was having just as much fun when Lola rolled her eyes and grabbed the voice changer from them.

"Lola, don't throw it away. Try it, go on, it feels funny," Jamie pleaded with Lola.

Lola put the voice changer in her pocket, picked up one of the boxes with the crazy-eyed animals in, and headed to the exit without saying a word to the two who were left astounded by her reaction. Lola normally liked a joke along with the next frog but when the nation's security is at stake, she put that first.

Jamie looked at Flapper.

Flapper looked at Jamie and said, "Oh, someone's tired."

"Lola, what's the matter, babe?" Jamie shouted after her.

"Agent J, come on. The Heron is getting away. And don't call me 'BABE'," Lola replied even more demandingly.

Jamie snapped into action. "Come on Flapper, what are you waiting for?"

Flapper stood in amazement at J's comment. "What do you mean waiting for? Lola's off her head if she thinks I'm chasing after The Heron if he is armed with the Ripper, J," Flapper added.

"Look Flapper, if we don't stop the Heron now, millions will be sent off to another dimension. Who knows where he will try to use it? Some may even get hurt in the process," Lola piped up, annoyed at the lack of enthusiasm from the other two.

"If we hurry we might be able to catch up with The Heron. He can't have got too far, besides I have bigger wings. I can fly faster than him any day of the week." Flapper became more focused again, focused on bringing the Heron down and ending the long ten-year campaign of tyranny.

"That's the spirit Flapper. Now let's get going." Lola seemed a bit happier now that she had her confidence back in the other two again.

CHAPTER 11 - PAUL & THE GREAT BIG BURP

Director Cod looked up from his green coloured laptop only to see Red standing over him, looking very worried about something.

"What is it Red? I'm a bit busy son."

"Umm well, Agents J and L have reported in. The Heron is back," Red replied.

"Well, we knew that Red, come on give me something to chew on." Cod was getting annoyed with Red's lack of common sense.

"Well, boss, the Heron has taken what we believe to be the human Ripper weapon and he has already used it on a section of dogs."

"What did you say Red? He has the Ripper?"

Red nodded at Cod after his comment.

"The Ripper was developed by a civilian contractor in the US to help remove the waste from our planet. The humans believed it could send their rubbish to a lifeless world of their choice such as Pluto or Jupiter."

Red interrupted Cod, "Look, I know what the Ripper does and why the humans decommissioned it before they even tested it. They had no control over it. We just need to focus on getting it back Boss."

"Ooh, get you. Finally, you found a bit of your brain to use, Red."

Red had been studying up on the humans ever since he graduated from the academy and even more so after being given his new position at C.F.I.A. He loitered in Cod's office, waiting for a reply to his outburst, but to no avail.

"Red, will that be all or is there a more pressing matter you have to deal with?" Cod eventually spoke.

Red walked over to the office door and turned to Cod to say something but stopped. He felt compelled to say something witty but couldn't think fast enough so instead he shook his head and exited a little more quickly than normal, embarrassed at his lack of wit.

Red moved through the shallow water of the headquarters main operations room with ease, creating swirls and mini whirlpools with his fins. The water lapped against tall cabinets housing television screens, radar monitors and various holographic tables. Red reached the far end of the room where the operations leader sat. He was surrounded by ten touch screen monitors and the tracking monitor. The monitor linked into satellite tracking, which automatically alerted the operations leader to any imminent terrorist attacks. The operations leader was a great big Bullfrog called...

"Paul, have you communicated with Agents J and L yet?" Red asked.

"CROAK." Paul cleared his throat and then began to talk, "Red, have you spoken to them yet? Because if you haven't spoken to them, that means I haven't been able to get a hold of them myself. Because you said to me fifteen minutes ago let me speak to J and L when they call in..."

"Alright Paul, I get the picture, calm down," Red replied.

Red turned away from the disgruntled bullfrog and headed toward the gadgets room.

Paul sucked in a deep breath, held it in for a bit and then, "BUUURRRRRRRRRRRRRPPPPP."

He let off the biggest burp he could find in himself, covering Red in the slimiest ball of stomach bile he had ever seen.

Paul sniggered at Red's misfortune.

"Arrgghh what do you think you're doing, Paul?" Red asked in disgust.

Paul did not answer. Instead, he gave a sly grin and turned back to his monitors. The other frogs and fish in the Agency were very jealous of what Red had achieved, just for being mates with one of the best field agents they had or that's what they thought anyway.

"This is Agent J, come in white tiger come in," White tiger was the radio code for C.F.I.A. headquarters.

"What is it J?" answered Paul.

"We need urgent backup. We've been pinned down outside the Salisbury plains east outer fence and.......... just hurry," Jamie demanded.

****

Whilst Red and Paul had been playing with snot balls, Jamie, Flapper, and Lola had bumped into a few straggling bald eagles who didn't turn and flee at the very mention of Jamie's name.

The eagles were swooping in with their long sharp talons bared, aiming for the intrepid trios' heads. Jamie couldn't see any way out of their tricky situation apart from calling in for reinforcements.

****

The Heron wasn't that far away from Jamie when he overheard him shouting down his communicator with his demands, between the cries of the bald eagles. He decided to turn around and try his new toy again but on something that deserved to be sent to another time or place. Well, in his mind, this was the right thing to do.

Frank stopped Heron mid turn. "Heron just think about what you are about to do. Jamie Pond doesn't even know we are here. We could just slip away and head straight for his headquarters in Tilgate as planned."

Heron paused for a little while. " I... I Guess you're right Frank."

Frank, Shifty and Heron all turned at the same time towards the deep thick of the woods. Frank grabbed a hold of Shifty and threw him on his back, and then shouted, "Hold on boy."

With that Frank and Heron launched into the early dusk sky, heading east towards Tilgate Park.

****

Jamie was throwing small sticks at the eagles, which had no effect at all. Flapper grabbed at branches still attached to trees, bending them back and trying to hit the eagles. One by one, Flapper was succeeding in stopping the eagles, shouting at Jamie and Lola as he did, "Get out, run!"

"But Flapper, we can't leave without you." Jamie protested.

"Jamie just go, I will be ok, NOW GO!" Flapper ordered this time.

Lola grabbed at Jamie's backpack handle and yanked him back towards the thick of the woods.

Deeper and deeper they ran into the woods, past the fences and firing ranges. The low-lying brambles and broken twigs at head height scratched at their smooth green skin. Well, head height to a frog is probably about eleven inches.

Jamie and Lola slowed to a light jog, looking for any breakaway eagles from the fight.

Lola said, panting trying to catch her breath, "Looks like Flapper managed to fend them off."

Jamie slumped to the woodland floor and held his head in his hands, trying to catch his own breath. "Flapper has to be the bravest bird I know."

"Jamie, I know, but he will be ok. Help is on the way. You heard the reply," Lola reassured Jamie.

Jamie raised his head from his hands and wiped the sweat from his brow. Grabbing the nearest fallen leaf he looked at Lola and uttered the words, "I've got to do it, Lola, I need a number two."

"Jamie what are you like!" Lola said, laughing. "Don't be long Jamie. We need to get moving."

"Ok Lola," Jamie replied.

****

No one had noticed the box that Flapper dropped during their fight with the bald eagles! The casing had shattered on one corner and a beam of light pierced through the split and hit the back of the box, scaring its inhabitant at first.

It had been a long time since the box dweller had seen any sort of light let alone daylight. The creature inside popped his velvety pink nose towards the beam of light. It felt warm to him at first, almost inviting. He could smell the freshly broken bracken and squashed grass that lay around his box. The undergrowth had left a green mush around the broken opening. When the creature licked this with his spiky and incredibly long tongue it left a bitter taste in his mouth. The creature moaned at first but then growled at the bitter green mush.

A squirrel hiding some acorns had seen the box fall and decided it might be a good place to store his nuts and acorns for the winter. The squirrel crept closer to the box, rocking back and forth like a chameleon stalking its prey. Closer he ventured until his nose poked through the new opening to the box. Sniffing the air inside he didn't see the furry arm extend out from the dark and then hit the bottom of the box. BANG! Just as the squirrel turned to run there was a squelch, and then a snap followed by a flash of fur and the squirrel was gone.

The creature smashed his head full force into the case, splitting the opening even more and allowing him enough room to crawl out through the hole. His crazy piercing yellow eyes bulged from their distended sockets, jumping around as they scanned through the tall trees and thick bracken. The creature had been engineered by scientists and had been deemed too terrible or just outright too **EVIL** and was never to be seen again, or that's what they had thought.

CHAPTER 12 - FROZEN DOG MESS SOUP

Lola called to Jamie to try to speed things up.

"JAMIE!" She shouted this time.

"Alright, look you can't rush a good poo now can you Lola," Jamie replied.

"Just hurry J."

Jamie stopped what he was doing and tilted his head to listen to something far away but muffled. *I hope Flappers ok,* he thought. Jamie finished his number two and rejoined Lola.

"You OK there Jamie you look lost me old fruitbat." Lola loved to mock Jamie. It was her favourite pastime.

"Look, I heard something."

"Yes?" asked Lola.

"No, listen. It's like something screaming in the distance, but not if you see what I mean."

"I thought you said listen. I can't see a sound dummy," Lola sniggered.

"You're not taking this seriously Lo…." Jamie stopped mid-sentence.

"No, you're right Jamie," Lola sniggered again.

"Oh, do you know what, forget it. It's probably just some poor defenseless squirrel being turned into a zombie but don't you worry your pretty little head about it," Jamie scolded Lola.

Lola ignored the last comment from J because her attention was on another noise, the noise of big flapping wings, a bit like Canadian goose wings beating together.

"Flapper, you made it," Lola shouted as Flapper emerged from the trees. "You look tired, but I'm sure carrying us back to headquarters won't be too much of a struggle for you," Lola added.

Flapper's heart pounded in his chest, and his beak was sore from his furious battle with the bald eagles. However, this hadn't deterred Flapper in the past, and it wasn't about to now. He turned his head to Lola and agreed to fly back to Tilgate.

Once again, the intrepid duo mounted Flappers back, strapped themselves in and waited for lift off.

Flapper took a deep breath and sighed before raising his wings ready for lift off. He thrust his wings hard on to the bracken covered ground, giving instant lift. The force was so strong it was enough to throw Lola and Jamie back into the harnessed seat.

"Get off me," Jamie shouted at Lola as they cleared the trees.

For her own amusement, Lola thrust her elbow into Jamie's stomach, winding him as she moved away.

Jamie looked down towards the clearing at the bunker. It looked peaceful and still until the soldiers appeared again, shattering the silence. He thought of the screaming, howls and whines like a pack of dogs crying out for help.

Jamie prodded the back of Lola's head with his long green index finger and then said, "Lola... Lola, I've got it."

"Got what Jamie?"

"The screaming. I know where I've heard it before."

Jamie paused when Lola turned her head to him.

"It's dogs, howling and whining. They sound lost, frightened and confused. Somewhere near but not if you see what I mean," Jamie said.

"Jamie what on earth are you...." Lola stopped as Flapper lulled again revealing more of the clearing. "What in god's name is that down there? Jamie Look... Look at it," Lola continued.

Jamie looked down again at the soldiers who had been bustling around the bunker entrance and were now gathering at what appeared to be a large pile of dog mess soup, frozen of course.

"Lola it looks like a big pile of dog's mess soup."

"Yeah but frozen," Lola added. "Jamie we need to get down there and get a sample before the humans contaminate the scene."

Flapper piped up. "If you think I'm landing down there near the soup then you have another thing coming my dears."

"Flapper, land down near the edge of the clearing in shelter of the trees. Jamie will handle it from there."

Jamie looked up and took note at Lola's comment to Flapper. "And when were you going to inform me of this? I do not think so missy. I'm not going anywhere near that!" Jamie protested.

"Look Flapper and Agent J, you will follow orders no matter what," Lola scolded again.

Jamie looked dismayed at the last comment. He didn't like taking orders from a girl but soon realised he had no choice but to agree with Lola.

Flapper nodded his head and began to descend back to the clearing, heading for the edge as ordered.

One of the soldiers saw Flapper's descent and panic set in as he remembered his earlier incident with The Heron.

"Oh My God, it's happening again RUN, RUN, RUN," the guard screamed at his comrades.

Somehow, the Ripper had failed to completely send the dogs to another dimension. They were just stuck in limbo and then reappeared as a pile of frozen soup.

Jamie could see the frozen mound when Flapper made his final approach towards the edge of the clearing. He grabbed at the opportunity to leap off of Flapper's back and land with a skid on top of the dog soup mound. Quickly grabbing his penknife, he cut a chunk off the mound and placed it into a plastic bag. He held his nose because the stench of frozen wet dog was overpowering to his tiny little nose.

The soldiers flapping around the frozen soup-like substance saw Jamie land. "Is that a frog? What's it doing?"

"Go on, get out of it," one of the guards shouted at Jamie.

However, little did they realise who they were dealing with.

Jamie looked up at the guards gathering around him and quickly grabbed at his communicator, touching the keypad. Two prongs shot out of the end. He jumped down to the ground and walked away from the frozen soup.

The guards, confused at the sight of a frog walking away from them on two legs shouted at Jamie. "Oi come here you little…"

Another guard shouted but soon stopped, frozen to the spot. Jamie had thrust his communicator's prongs into the ground and fired it. A paralyzing shockwave shot through the ground. Just as the shockwave hit Jamie jumped up clear of the ground and balanced for a moment on the end of the communicator, and then made a bolt for Flapper and Lola.

Jamie found Flapper waiting at the edge of the forest and mounted him again. "Did you get it, Jamie?" Lola asked in a firm but soft voice.

Jamie thrust the bag into Lola's face and smiled, holding the slightly defrosted bag of dog mess soup.

Jamie put the plastic bag in his rucksack and settled into Flapper's harness, closing his eyes for the journey home. Lola settled in too, ready for the journey.

Flapper took off less urgently than before and circled around the clearing for a little while, making sure The Heron was not hanging around, before heading back to Tilgate.

CHAPTER 13 - MR DROOL

Shifty took one look at the Heron's evil grin. "Heron what are you so happy about, J got away again."

"Look Shifty, like I said earlier, I have big plans for him. I want to see him suffer."

"Yeah, but he probably knows why we attacked the base and what we took from there."

"Yes dear boy, but you fail to see the bigger picture, Shifty."

"And what would that be, Heron?" Shifty was even more puzzled at the Heron's taunts.

"I will enlighten you," Heron replied, rolling his sinister eyes.

"Firstly, J doesn't understand the real potential of the Ripper. He will find out soon enough, because we will be ready for him, waiting silently in the dark of the forest around the silt lake." The Heron continued, "Secondly, agent Lola will be separated from J on a false tip-off. Away from Lola, J is useless. He needs her to back him up."

"You have it all planned out, don't you Heron? Does mummy know about these plans yet or are you going to go at this one alone," Shifty added.

"Oh, do shut up Shifty," Heron blurted out rather hurriedly.

Frank circled overhead, catching the thermals rising from the plains next to the Porton Down facility, watching out for J or anybody else who might try to hinder the Heron's plans. After a good ten minutes of circling, he descended back down to the dark of the forest, only to find the Heron had already moved deeper into it.

Shifty had paused for a short while, waiting for Frank to stop circling and arrive, but decided to run off and try to catch up with the Heron.

He searched through the dense forest but couldn't find any sign of The Heron, and gingerly landed on some damp moss which had grown on top of a fallen tree. The moss felt cold and wet under his claws, making him shiver when he settled. Shifty hopped over to the next pile of moss, peering through fallen branches and looking for his boss when all of a sudden out of nowhere a snarling growling row of teeth popped up through the branches. Startled, he fell backwards onto the wet moss, the teeth moving closer and closer until he could feel the hot doggy breath and sticky saliva dripping onto his beak.

Shifty clamped his eyes shut, waiting to be eaten in one swift foul swoop when he felt the rough of a wet slobbery tongue lick his feathery face. The lick left both Shifty and the slobbering dog uncomfortable as the dog now had a mouth full of speckled feathers.

He stood up, brushed himself down and saw the teeth again, only this time it had a tongue hanging out of them dripping and wavering around in a frenzy as its owner was panting rather excitedly.

"And what would your name be me old slobber-puss."

Shifty waited patiently for an answer. But all he got was an excited bark. What Shifty didn't know was that the dog was the only survivor of the dog mess soup. Frozen of course! The dog had survived the journey from one universe to the next without a scratch apart from a slightly lowered IQ. Really, there was no harm done at all.

Shifty looked at the slobbering canine and said, "Come on Mr. Drool, let's go and find The Heron. You can give me a lift."

Shifty hopped onto the back of the dog and held on tightly. He kicked with his heel just as a champion jockey would at the off on a daring steeplechase.

The dog turned and bounded over the undergrowth, pushing through bushes and low-lying branches of great tall oaks. Shifty felt every leap and bound as they traversed through the dark woods.

A few minutes of running had passed when Shifty shouted at the dog to slow down, just before they reached a clearing. He could see shadows moving around in the clearing and wanted to make sure it wasn't Agent J and his team.

Mr. Drool slowed to a gentle but silent walk towards the clearing. He stooped his head down as if stalking prey in the tall grasses of an African plain.

The Heron had decided to set up camp in a clearing a few hundred metres away from the bunker. The Ripper was rather heavy for his frail wings to carry.

"Frank," The Heron called. "We will rest here until dawn when we will make haste to Tilgate and call on Agent J and his so-called C.F.I.A."

There were shouts of excitement and anger from the hollering henchmen around him.

The Heron preached to his minions, "We will strike fear into the hearts of our enemy and aim the ripper at Tilgate Park." The Heron became louder and louder as he reveled in his dastardly plan. He continued, "Nothing will stand in our way. They will hand over Agent J. They dare not take any risk that we might wipe out the entire park with the Ripper, sending all of its inhabitants to another universe."

Shifty had reached the opening by this time and heard everything that the Heron was planning. He leaned down to Mr. Drool's ear, tugged it back and whispered, "Come on we're off. I didn't agree to any of that when he asked me to help. I was just here to pick some locks."

Mr. Drool tilted his head to one side then the other, nodded, and slowly turned away from the clearing, leaving the Heron ranting on at his minions.

Shifty whispered again, to himself, "I can't believe I'm going to do what I'm going to do next."

Mr. Drool looked back at Shifty, waiting for his directions. "Best speed to Tilgate, my slobbery friend."

Now Tilgate is about four hours by goose and five hours by Pigeon. By dog, oh my that's a good eight hours hard running. Shifty had a long ride ahead of him.

CHAPTER 14 - JAMIE & THE PUMP HOUSE

Jamie, Lola and Flapper had reached the edge of Farnborough just as dark clouds started to gather around them, making the air cool a little.

"Jamie, Lola, we need to rest for a little while, we can carry on again in the morning." Flapper didn't demand but expected the duo to comply.

Both Jamie and Lola looked at each other and nodded, agreeing with their feathery pal.

"Good that's settled then." Flapper circled overhead for a little while until he was satisfied with a secluded rest stop. Flapper spotted it, he swooped down towards a water pump station just south of the M3 motorway and just before Junction 4. He turned into the wind then out and then back in again until finally touching down next to the front door of the pump house.

Jamie piped up, "Excuse me please; I am an expert in the picking of locks. Watch and learn as I crack this one."

Lola sniggered at J's comment. "An expert at picking your nose don't you mean."

Jamie took one look at Lola and shrugged his shoulders. He then carried on to the door and prepared to unlock it.

Jamie swung his backpack off his shoulders and let it fall to the ground. He selected his small climbing suction cups from inside the bag, placing one on each of his smooth hands and then one on each knee.

"Now, Jamie if you had been born as a tree frog you wouldn't need the suckers!" Lola sniggered again.

Tutting as he did so he grabbed for his lock picks. By this time Flapper had already carried Lola over to the door and lifted her up to the handle, only to find it already open.

"Don't tell him Flapper, this will be funny," Lola whispered and pointed down to Jamie stumbling over his own feet with suction cups stuck fast to the smooth concrete in front of the door.

Flapper couldn't hold it any longer, and pushed the door open, much to Jamie's dismay. "You did that on purpose, didn't you Lola?"

"Yep," Lola replied at Jamie's scowl.

Lola and Flapper stepped over the unfortunate fool stuck to the floor, looking a little like a fly stuck to flypaper, bobbing up and down.

Lola said to Flapper, "Leave the poor dear there. It will teach him a lesson."

The evening was drawing in now. Dew was settling on nearby meadow grass surrounding the pump house, and the crisp summer leaves of the trees. Spider webs glistened, and Jamie's nose was wetter than ever.

He was beginning to wish he had not asked for the suction cups, which had Velcro on the back of them that wrapped around your limbs. The Velcro was starting to chafe on his knees.

"LOLA, come on, let me go, please," Jamie pleaded.

Not more than a minute passed and Jamie could hear laughing from within in the pump house. Jamie scowled even more at this, but just then Lola poked her head around the open door and sniggered at the sight of Jamie stuck frog again.

He looked up at Lola, staring at her with his big yellow bulbous eyes and said nothing as she continued to snigger.

Lola did eventually release Jamie from the suction cups and offered him some comforting hot chocolate she had whipped up from her backpack, and warmed on a small campfire she had prepared earlier in between sniggering.

Jamie finally settled down with Lola and Flapper at the campfire, watching the shadows dance around the vaulted ceiling of the deserted pump control room.

Flapper stretched out a feathery hand to Jamie and patted him on the shoulders, "No hard feelings mate. It's just you did look a bit silly bobbing up and down on the concrete."

Jamie didn't comment, he just gave a disapproving look and shook his head before lying down, using his backpack as a pillow.

Flapper turned to Lola, shrugged his shoulders and ruffled his feathers. He tucked his head under his wing, keeping one eye exposed just in case of any intruders or humans.

Jamie drifted off quickly straight into a dream state. In his dream, he jumped from lily pad to lily pad in slow motion. At first, he was like a feather drifting in the wind with a cheesy grin spreading from ear to ear, as if he was looking at a vast bounty of roast flies and toasted crickets. Although this sounds, quite disgusting flies and crickets to a frog are just like chocolate and jelly bear sweets to you and me. Jamie's drifting in slow motion began to quicken slightly. The grin was now more of a smile and then a frown.

His jumping from pad to pad generated small waves as he leapt. The sky above him became darker in waves like dark rain clouds in a storm. In the distance, someone shouted his name repeatedly, never stopping until it became so loud he woke, jumping up from his sleep and crashing straight into Flapper's left wing.

In reality, Jamie had been asleep for about five hours, which was just enough time for the Heron's crows to circle around overhead looking for them.

The crows had seen the flickering of the orange flames from within the pump house and attacked at dawn, catching Flapper and Lola by surprise. They both jumped into action as wave after wave of crows came crashing through the pump house door.

Jamie had jumped from his sleep just as Flapper caught the last crow trying to peck at Jamie's face. Lola had been shouting at Jamie as the crows were coming in. She had managed to grab a smouldering stick from the fire to beat off the attackers. She slumped down to the ground, threw her now broken stick down, and grabbed at her arm, breathing heavily. She looked down at her forearm to see a long gash in her purple skin. Jamie tore off a piece of his shirt and began wrapping it around her wound. Lola gave him an approving smile as he dressed the gash. She grimaced as he tied it tightly around her arm to stop the steady flow of blood.

All three sat on the cold floor, silent at first.

Jamie was the first to speak. "The Heron is still close then."

Lola took one look at Jamie, then at Flapper. Shaking her head, she replied, "What do you think, brain ache?"

Jamie scowled at Lola's comment but quickly withdrew and smiled back, realising his dopey comment.

After he got his breath back, Flapper spoke to both of them. "Guys we need to get moving, Cod will be waiting for our report and we need to avoid The Heron's henchmen as he's bound to send more out looking for us."

Both Jamie and Lola nodded and agreed with Flapper and off they went, not looking back.

CHAPTER 15 - BEST CLAW FORWARD

The Heron stomped up and down his lair, huffing and puffing as he did so.

He stopped at each end of his makeshift base, tutting with every turn before he carried on walking again. Frank followed his movements just like a spectator at a tennis match. He stopped himself and shook his head and commented on the antics of the Heron.

He decided enough was enough. "Heron, when are we going to attack Agent J's headquarters?" Frank was becoming very agitated at the waiting around. He was an action bird, best claw forward and all that nonsense.

"Look, frankly Frank, I don't care how long we wait. The timing has to be right. If J isn't there   everything we have fought for stands for nothing." The Heron was disappointed in Frank's impatience.

"Then why are you stomping around Heron. It's annoying," Frank replied.

A few more moments of tutting went by when one of the crows that attacked our heroes returned to the Heron. Catching his breath, he told of the failed mission, offering no comfort to the Heron at all. However, after the small battle the crow waited, hiding in some trees above the pump house. He was watching for J and the others and which direction they would travel in and just as he thought, they were headed straight back to Tilgate, to headquarters. The Heron was now most pleased with this news and could not wait to tell Frank that he could finally have his moment and take down the C.F.I.A.

****

Little did The Heron know or anyone else for that matter that Jamie had already anticipated this and sent a text message to Red explaining his fears as they were leaving the pump house.

Red had immediately put the wheels into motion, calling all agents to tell them to assemble at the emergency headquarters in a nearby village called Colgate. The tunnels used by Jamie earlier also lead straight to the emergency HQ, under a church at the centre of Colgate, deep within its hidden vaults. Once everyone is assembled inside the tunnel is sealed with six foot thick lead shutters. If intruders compromise the original HQ, the complex will go into meltdown, destroying all sensitive data and materials and leaving nothing behind.

Flapper shouted back at Jamie and Lola, "We're nearly at Tilgate. Hold on guys."

"No, wait!" Jamie shouted back.

Flapper turned his head mid-flight back at Jamie. "Why?... What?... Do you have something better in mind?"

"Yes. Drop me at Tilgate and take yourself and Lola on to Colgate to the other HQ."

Flapper did not like the thought of leaving Jamie at Tilgate in the hands of fate. "No, Jamie. I'll stay with you, what have you got planned?"

Lola butted in, "You're not dropping me at Colgate to miss any action. I'm staying and that's that."

Jamie knew there was no point in arguing with them, especially Lola, so he shrugged his shoulders and nodded at the pair of them. "We wait for the Heron at HQ in Tilgate near the secondary entrance in the officers' mess."

Jamie carried on explaining his plan, making sure nothing was overlooked.

He planned to lead The Heron into Headquarters through the back entrance and escape through the front, as this would only activate for agents of the C.F.I.A. The entrance would then seal, leaving The Heron and his henchmen trapped in the complex. The countdown would start for the meltdown procedure. There was only a thirty second timer on this, leaving Jamie and Lola possibly trapped as well.

Satisfied that Lola and Flapper understood what had to be done, and the short amount of time to do it in Jamie decided it was time. Time for another poo. When you have to go you have to go. Jamie liked nothing more than having a good poo. It was at these times that his mind would focus on things more clearly.

****

The Heron, Frank and a thousand other birds were edging closer and closer to Tilgate. Frank lumbered with the Ripper as he was the strongest amongst them all.

****

Red waited patiently for word from Jamie of the entrapment of the Heron and his henchman.

****

Shifty and the slobber machine, in the meantime, were bounding towards Tilgate as fast as they could go. That is until they hit a clearing in the heart of Warnham Park where Mr. Drool stopped and skidded across the damp dewy grass like a footballer sliding in for a deep tackle. The dog came to a halt and lay on his side, looking at something that terrified him.

Thrown into the air Shifty caught a low level branch. He hung there looking, staring at the same terrifying thing that Mr. Drool was looking at.

Shifty and Mr. Drool had stumbled across a creature which resembled a squirrel but it was as if somebody had supersized it.

Its eyes were bulging out of proportion with its head. The forearms were elongated with massive shovel like hands and claws that could tear open a solid steel door. Its body was about the same size as a Jack Russell and it had a tail the same length and size as a large fox's tail. All in all quite a powerful squirrel indeed.

Mr. Drool slowly stood up to try to walk away from it but as he did so the branch Shifty was holding onto snapped, sending him crashing down to the wet grass and giving him the most uncomfortable feeling. The noise of the branch snapping startled the super sized squirrel. Mr. Drool had to duck as the squirrel pushed him to the ground, using him to thrust its body harder and escaping the unlikely new friends. Shifty could only watch as the thing disappeared into the undergrowth of nearby trees.

"What was that?" Shifty looked at a blank expression from his four-legged friend. "Oh who am I kidding. Come on Mr. Drool. Let's get to Tilgate. I know their headquarters is there somewhere."

Mr. Drool looked and tilted his head to one side then back again. Tongue hanging out and flopping up and down, he nodded at Shifty and lowered his back for him to jump on. Shifty and Mr. Drool carried on with their journey, racing against time, trying to beat The Heron to warn Jamie and the others.

CHAPTER 16 - COUNTDOWN TO MELTDOWN

Inside the flight officers mess at the C.G.A.F., Jamie, Flapper and Lola sat drinking strawberry milkshakes, as cool as cucumbers, waiting for the Heron. They started talking about the Ripper and its untold power.

Jamie reached over the table they were sitting at, looking for Lola's bag. He had seen the voice changer poking out of one pocket. Before Lola could stop him he grabbed it and jumped back just out of webbed hands reach.

Jamie sniggered as he switched it on. "HA HA TOO LATE. I HAVE THE DEVICE NOW."

Lola gave a disappointed look at Jamie and nudged Flapper in the ribs because he was at this point in full stomach cramp eye watering laughter.

"How can you two joke at a time like this?" Lola continued. "The Heron is nearly upon us and all you can think of is mucking around, you're like kids the pair of you." Lola wasn't at all happy with their carefree attitude.

****

The Heron was gaining more ground with every minute that went by. Hastily they flew with southeasterly winds helping push them faster than ever.

They had now reached Horsham, below them Frank could see tall pines and vast oaks painting the countryside. One by one, the ravens were zipping past Frank as he tired from carrying the Ripper all the way from Salisbury.

"HERON," Frank shouted out towards the front of the flocks of ravens, crows, and eagles.

The Heron didn't hear Frank at first, until he shouted a second time. Dropping back, he glided with his impressive wingspan next to Frank.

"What's the problem, Frank?"

"I need to have a breather. This really is heavy you know."

Heron flapped a few times to keep the momentum going. "Well seeing as you have carried it all this way and we are very nearly at our destination..." The Heron paused for a few seconds and then said, "No."

He resumed his position at the head of the hordes. Heron pointed at the birds to his left and right and shouted, "ON MY LEFT FLY SOUTH, ON MY RIGHT FLY EAST AS PLANNED."

The heron had earlier laid out his plan to his new flocks. A section would fly in from the south of Tilgate, and another section would fly in from the east a few moments later surprising the C.F.I.A., or that's what he thought.

Frank picked up a good thermal from an exposed area just north of Colgate, pushing him higher above the hordes of flocking birds. He drew his wings back and rocketed towards the front of the flock like a heat-seeking missile. He quickly stretched out his wing tips, slowing him down as he came alongside The Heron.

"Are we nearly there yet Heron?"

"Oh, you're just like a kid Frank."

"Heron old buddy, I really can't hold on to this for much longer. I'm going to drop it."

Heron looked back at the remaining birds in his section and saw two huge ravens flying just proud of the others. "Hold on Frank."

Heron dropped back to the two ravens. "Hey guys, you look like good strong birds. Go and relieve the old man up front there from his load."

The ravens were intimidated by the very presence of The Heron, even though they could obviously take care of themselves. They agreed and accelerated to the front with

Frank. "Here, let us take that off you, it looks really heavy."

Frank replied, "Did Heron put you two up to this?"

The ravens smiled at each other, then took the Ripper from Frank. *Oh, what a relief,* he thought. Frank quickened his pace, keeping up with the more agile of the invasion forces.

With Crawley in sight now, The Heron was getting anxious at his impending battle with his archenemy Agent J.

Some of the birds flew south of Gatwick and approached Tilgate from the east. The Heron pulled up slightly from his group and signaled for everyone to land on a roundabout just on the outskirts of Crawley and Colgate.

The Heron watched his army of birds flock to the roundabout like a deep dark storm cloud. Passersby stopped and looked up at the sky to see it had blackened slightly like a solar eclipse. Swirling round and around the dark hordes swooped onto the roundabout. The Heron looked at the cars crashing into each other, steam whistled from crumpled radiators and busy workers in nearby factories stopped what they were doing to take a look at the ominous cloud of feathers.

A cyclist slowed to look at the swirling mass of terror and careered into the path of an oncoming raven. The cyclist coughed and spluttered at his mouthful of feathers. Fearful of the mass of birds people started to emerge from their cars but were too scared to venture away, watching in awe at the sight of so many birds in one place.

The Heron carried on speaking at the gathering horde. "Everyone pay attention. I will not repeat this. We wait here for the signal from the first attackers and then we will swoop in and strike again when the C.F.I.A. least expect it."

"When do we go on strike?" one of the ravens piped up from the middle of the flock.

"I'm going to ignore that comment you imbecile," The Heron replied.

Onwards the first section flew, getting closer and closer to their goal. The sky was becoming quite dark now as the evening started to draw in. Long dark shadows crept across the ground as the sun began to set behind the South Downs. People busied themselves with their mishaps from the earlier swirling tornado of birds.

The Heron looked all around at the flapping humans taking pictures of the birds sitting, standing, and flapping every now and then. He decided it was nearly time to go on.

"Frank dear boy prepare the RIPPER." The Heron stopped.

In the distance you could hear a faint noise a bit like the birdy song. Suddenly the Heron grabbed at his side under his right wing to try to stop his mobile phone from reciting any more of the birdy song. The birds all erupted in riotous laughter at the Heron's ring tone.

"STOP!" the Heron shouted. "Just STOP!" he shouted again.

Even the humans stopped at this point. "This could be word from the first section." Even more frustrated than ever the Heron answered his phone.

Frank jumped up from his perch and began to wave his wings around like a crazed rabid peacock. The people who were hanging around were certainly not hanging around for long after his little outburst. There were people tripping over each other and jumping over cars. Some just calmly opened their car doors, stepped in and then closed and pushed the lock, not looking over at the Heron, trying not to draw attention to themselves.

It was now the birds turn, to stand and stare in awe at the sight of so many people running scared, this same sight sparked a dark thought in The Herons brain. It was so evil, so dark that Frank could see the look on his face. The Heron started sliding across the slippery grass, edging towards the ravens holding the Ripper.

"NO!" Frank shouted. He launched at The Heron, grabbing his wings. "No. Not this time Heron. Save it for later. Our fight is not with them, it's with J and Lola."

The Heron knew Frank was right and withdrew his feathery hand from the Ripper. "Sorry Frank. Got a bit carried away there then."

Heron grabbed at his phone again. A text message had been left by the first section: WE HAVE MADE IT BUT EVERYONE HAS GONE PLEASE ADVISE. The Heron was a bit despondent at this news and ordered his flock to fly like the wind to Tilgate. He would follow closely behind. With a mass of feathers and dust the flock launched up off the roundabout and headed east again towards Tilgate.

****

Jamie and his companions lay quietly inside the flight officers mess listening to the birds fumbling around the lake, not having the intelligence to realise it was a trap and they were all about to be wiped out.

Jamie reached over to Lola and patted her on the shoulder, then whispered, "Lola what do you think? I can't see The Heron anywhere. He isn't with them. Do you think he may be waiting elsewhere?"

Lola turned to Jamie, placed her smooth green finger to her lips, uttered a sigh and shushed him.

Jamie couldn't help but wonder what the Heron was up to. Had he figured out Jamie's plan? Did he already know about the failsafe protocols installed at headquarters? He shook his head and said aloud, "Nah I don't think so."

"SHUSH!" Lola silenced him again.

Flapper poked his head up from their hiding place only to see twenty or so ravens and a few crows standing at the edge of the lake banks, waiting for something or someone to arrive. Flapper snapped his head around to see a black shadow swooping in from the west in front of the setting sun.

Jamie grabbed at Lola's arm, pulling her back out of view. Jamie knew the black shadow was either The Heron or one of the bald eagles flying in.

He poked his head out of the flight officers' mess for a quick peek at the shadow again. He looked around to the left and right before looking up at a big grey body perched on tall gangly dark legs. He slowly withdrew himself from the opening, hoping and praying that The Heron hadn't heard his movements.

Unfortunately for Jamie, Frank had landed a few metres opposite the opening and could see Jamie's head poking out of the mess room. Frank was carrying the Ripper again and was now trying with all his might to alert The Heron with hand gestures and head bobbing, but couldn't make the Heron understand what he was gesturing at.

"What on earth are you doing Frank? You look like you are doing the Highland fling dear boy." The Heron tilted his head to one side and then shook it, looking down at the same time. Heron couldn't believe what he was seeing, and soon realised what Frank had been trying to say to him. The Heron's eyes bulged out in utter awe of the sight of a little green pair of feet disappearing into the large opening in the side of the bank.

"That's what I was trying to tell you!" Frank dropped his head and buried it into his feathery hand.

As quick as The Heron could turn and reach down to grab the little green feet they disappeared. Heron crouched down to look into the opening but jumped back quickly when he saw Frank aim the Ripper at the entrance. Frank without thinking pressed the trigger, but there was nothing, not even a clunk or a fizz from the digital read out. Frank tried again but with no luck. Until he started to turn it around to look into the barrel of the ripper. Just as he turned it the ripper fired, the shock wave sent Frank flying backwards into the watery outcrops of the lake.

The Heron stood still for a few seconds, watching and waiting for something to happen. Again nothing. The Ripper had fired off into the atmosphere, sending a few mosquitoes off to oblivion and the odd moth, but there was no serious harm done to anyone or anything.

"Frank, what are you playing at? You could have hit me then."

"Sorry Heron. I got a bit trigger happy." He paused before adding, as The Heron bolted upright, "Come on guys, we are right on top of the secret headquarters. Everyone this way."

The Heron gestured with his hands at the entrance to the flight officer's mess.

Jamie and Lola had obviously fled to the lower tunnels by now, drawing in the birds deep to their doom.

The Heron wasn't stupid. He knew about the security protocols as he had tried this once before when Jamie's Dad was still head of section 'S'. Frank jumped up from his crouched position behind some hawthorn bushes and gave chase, following behind the rest of the Heron's small army.

"Whoa, whoa and........ whoa Frank calm down, easy does it." The Heron held aloft a feathery hand like a traffic officer at a busy junction. Frank stopped dead in his tracks and snapped his head round to see The Heron's evil smile beaming from ear to ear.

****

Jamie and Lola had gathered quite a bit of speed, hopping and bounding towards the emergency tunnel exit. The tunnel exit was situated between the main control room and the gadget sciences room, but wasn't very easy to get to as there were obstacles everywhere on the way to this point. The only saving grace with this tunnel was that it has face recognition to save time in an emergency, like the emergency they had at hand.

Jamie paused for a second in the control room, looking around for any stragglers from the earlier evacuation.

Lola grabbed at Jamie. "COME ON!" she shouted. "The countdown has already started. We need to go."

Jamie swung his whole body round towards the emergency tunnel door and leaped again.

"30 .... 29....28....27....26," came from four big loudspeakers in the corners of the control room. Jamie could hear the approaching minions squawking and cackling as they too blundered their way through the cluttered headquarters.

"25….24….23….22….21." Again the countdown loomed over them.

Jamie and Lola had reached the exit door but before they could stand in front of the facial recognition camera, two of the birds broke free from the rabble and gained more ground than the others. They grabbed at Lola, missed, stumbled, and then tried again. One bird caught Lola's jacket, ripping it at the seams as she pulled away.

"NO!" Lola shouted, then turned and grabbed but her hand slipped away from the jacket.

Meanwhile, Jamie had managed to get the camera to work on his face. Pausing for a few seconds the door banged and then sprang into life, it juddered as it started to rise from its mountings. It raised a few inches but then stuck in the runners, then a few more inches and jammed again. There was just enough room to squeeze a small bird and a smooth purple and yellow tree frog through the tight gap. Jamie spun Lola to the floor, flinging her under the door. She yelped as she spun under, scraping her shoulder as she flew through the gap. Lola stopped when she was the other side of the door and reached out for Jamie but as she did, the door slammed shut, trapping Jamie in with the birds.

"JAMIE, NO!" Lola screamed at the top of her voice.

"15... 14.... PLEASE EVACUATE THE BUILDING. THIS FACILITY IS SET TO SELF DESTRUCT... 11."

Panic started to set in with Jamie. The last few seconds felt like an eternity to him until he remembered his ride to the officers' mess. The birds that had given chase were now scrambling and scraping at the closed door. Feathers were flying everywhere. The two birds that had caught up with Jamie and Lola now joined the mass of feathers. Jamie calmly walked over, past the mound of feathery bodies and on towards the touch screen in the wall. "10...9...8." The countdown carried on counting.

Jamie placed his hand on the touch screen panel. Amazingly the door shot up, allowing him time to dive into the tunnel.

"6...5...4...3....2...1." There was a pause for a few seconds, giving the birds false hope. However, not for long. There was a loud bang and then flames engulfed the main control room, destroying everything in the fiery wake.

Lola had managed to scramble for the safety of the lily pads in the middle of the lake. She lay there a few minutes, head in hands and sobbing at Jamie's suspected demise. Flapper had managed to escape the officers' mess when The Heron's back was turned. He was circling above, watching and waiting for Jamie and Lola to emerge from the depths of the lake, but when he only saw Lola his heart sank into his stomach. He flew down towards the edge of the lake and landed on the bank nearest Lola's lily pad. He reached out for Lola but she withdrew from him.

The Heron, Frank, and a few stragglers had fled the scene a little before time ran out, heading towards a nearby church. The Heron was laughing uncontrollably as he approached the church, imagining the end of Jamie Pond and the beginning of a new era. Snatch had waited around for a bit to see if there were any survivors of the blast, but when he only saw Lola emerge from the lake he jumped for joy. The hairs on the back of his neck stood on end causing a shiver to run down his spine. *Have to tell the Heron*, he thought.

The resulting blast from the security protocols caused a breach in the control room walls. At first water rushed into the control room, extinguishing the flames before they could destroy all living things in there. The birds panicked at the water filled room but soon the panic turned to terror as the water suddenly reversed back through the breach. The birds were scrabbling over each other, trying to swim away from the hole in the wall, as there was no telling what would happen to them on the other side. Unfortunately, the water was too strong and sucked all of the birds through the hole anyway.

Lola and Flapper looked frantically around in the splashing of water from the flapping birds trying to swim and scramble onto lily pads dotted around the lake.

"He isn't there, is he Flapper?" Lola looked dismayed as she asked the question.

Flapper ignored her and carried on searching until he noticed a rat hopping up and down in frenzy and then running off in the direction of the church.

"Quick Lola. I know where the Heron is and he's going to pay for this." Flapper extended one of his wings to Lola for her to jump on.

CHAPTER 17 - THE CLEVER FROG

The Heron was feeling rather safe and satisfied with his dastardly plan. He turned to Frank, smiled and then grabbed the Ripper from him. He pointed it at Frank.

"What are you doing?" Frank started edging away from The Heron who was now cackling and growling uncontrollably.

"You're mad, Heron." Frank tried to crouch behind a church pew whilst the Heron held aloft the Ripper, laughing harder and deeper than ever before.

"Frank, dear boy I'm only joking. Did you really think I would use this against my best friend?"

Frank raised his head above the back of the pew, peering over to The Heron. "I really did think you were going to pull the trigger then, Heron."

"Don't be silly Frank. Although I did think better of you though, never mind. Look Frank, I'm excited that Agent J has been destroyed. The C.F.I.A. have been wiped out. I feel like a million pounds right now."

"Heron don't count your chickens yet. Agent L escaped the blast," Frank replied.

The Heron walked up the aisle of the church, admiring his reflection in the polished brass ornaments uniformly placed around the church. You could tell the Clergyman of this church was a proud man.

"Frank, dear boy, I have every expectation that Lola and that daft bird of theirs will not be joining us at any moment. Snatch has already sent a message, telling me they are on their way. So I decided to send him in the opposite direction, they are bound to follow him thinking he will lead them to us," Heron said. "Follow him... Follow him do you really think they are that stupid Heron," Frank replied.

The Heron beckoned for Frank to walk over to a stained glass window in the south-west corner of the church. It had a picture of St. Christopher carrying a baby across a wide ocean. Just below the effigy's feet was a transparent part of the glass about six inches across and as many high.

Frank crept over to the window, leaned forward to the small peephole, and stood there aghast at the sight of a Canadian goose flapping off into the distance with a small figure perched on the back of it.

There was a slight pause before The Heron spoke. "See, I told you." The Heron looked very smug about his little plan.

Frank had to agree. "You really are that devious aren't you?"

The Heron gave a smug smile at the ferocious bird of prey that was still reeling from the sight of Flapper flying in the opposite direction.

Lola and Flapper had already seen Snatch divert off into the church graveyard, thinking he had given them the slip.

Flapper looked back over his left wing and gestured to the church.

"Yes, let's do it, Flapper," Lola said.

Satisfied with Lola's response Flapper tilted his left wing down towards the treetops and spun around 180 degrees, facing directly towards the church. He picked up a bit of speed, diving in hard like a golden eagle swooping in for his prey.

Flapper's eyes were hurting as he strained to see, cutting through the air like a stealth plane. Lola was clinging on for dear life as he approached faster and faster towards the large stained glass window at the head of the church a few hundred feet away.

Flapper closed his eyes and shouted back to Lola, "THIS IS REALLY GOING TO HURT LOLA!"

"Don't you worry about me," she shouted back. "Just get us inside that church," she added.

Lola hugged tightly to Flappers back, waiting for the impact of the glass. Just for a second she popped her head up to see how close they were but quickly withdrew it as Flapper, Lola, and millions of shards of stained glass came crashing through the window, into the church.

Luckily, Flapper had headed straight for a pile of old kneeling cushions waiting for the pastor to lay them in front of the pews.

The Heron didn't even have time to turn as Flapper and Lola came crashing through. He had been thrown back by

Flapper's speed, and an incredibly strong wing striking him in the face.

Flapper nursed a cut on his left wing and brushed off some of the rubble that had been dislodged when they burst through the stained glass window.

A few moments passed and The Heron came to, to find Lola standing over him holding a pair of handcuffs, ready to take him in. She had managed to scramble out of the cushions quickly enough to catch The Heron while he was still dazed.

Frank, however, was standing back out of the way when the kamikaze pair came crashing through the window. Frank held aloft the Ripper and pointed it at Lola's small body.

"LOLA!" Frank shouted.

She turned her head towards the shout only to see a burst of light racing towards her. Thinking quickly, she dove into the Herons ruffled feathers and clung on tightly. *If I'm going you're going too,* she thought, wincing at the impending impact.

The light beam passed over Lola's back, catching a few of The Heron's feathers. His feathers sizzled from the cold icy blast of light. He then grabbed Lola by her hind legs and held her hanging upside down in midair.

Squirming in discomfort she said, "Put me down, you brute."

The Heron laughed at her request as Frank joined them from the corner. "Sorry Heron, I saw Lola standing there and couldn't resist using the Ripper against her."

Flapper opened one eye and saw Lola being held against her will by the Heron. He decided to do nothing yet with the pair of them, together they were more than a match for him even with his greater strength and size. The Heron on his own he could handle. All he had to do was distract Frank long enough to take out the Heron and then grab Lola before escaping through the arched front doors.

The church was quite large with high vaulted ceilings and gargoyles looking down menacingly at the rows of pews, their snarls transfixed as they watched the humans gather aimlessly every Sunday morning. In every alcove there was a stained glass window picturing fables and events from the bible.

Flapper knew he would have a hard task on his hands to grab Lola and get out before Frank realised anything was amiss. He sat, contemplating, for a few more moments and watched as Snatch appeared from behind one of the old oak panels lining the lower half of the walls.

"Well, Snatch, just what were you thinking? You led them right here," The Heron told his small furry friend.

"You asked me to divert them, and that's what I did. I didn't know they had seen me turn around in the village green."

"Oh, do shut up Snatch you whine too much."

"But Heron."

"No Snatch, drop it. I have Lola now and can't decide what to do with her."

Frank whispered something in The Heron's ear, then turned to Snatch, pointed and then turned back to The Heron. They both gave a sinister laugh with their backs to Snatch. Frank lifted his left wing slightly and again came a burst of light, but this time more accurate. Snatch disappeared into a cloud of dust. The very fabric of space around him distorted into a vortex, sucking everything into its centre.

When the dust settled, Snatch had gone and also half a pew where he had been standing. A small bowl shape had formed in the once polished oak flooring, exposing a bit of the screed floor underneath. Cold steam rose from the newly formed bowl shape.

Lola hadn't seen the true potential of the Ripper until now and started panicking at the thought of the same thing happening to her.

****

Meanwhile, back at the devastated headquarters Red was in search of survivors of the blast, and more importantly his best pal Jamie Pond. This was more than difficult, as most of the structure had caved in on itself. Water cascaded down into the ruined headquarters making the search efforts ever more difficult. Red carried on searching anyway, Cod joining his determined counterpart in the search. But they found nothing and no one anywhere in the remains and not even infrared cameras could detect any warm bodies under the rubble, not that this would have any effect with Jamie of course but let's not tell them that.

Red stopped everyone by raising his fin. He reached down into what seemed like a small cave in the rubble and pulled out a rucksack and jacket from within, but no sign of its owner.

Suddenly he knew who these belonged to and felt a little bit of hope for his best friend's survival.

Cod grabbed hold of Red's dorsal fin. "Don't worry my scaly green friend, he will have figured a way out of the blast. He's a clever frog."

Red gave Cod a disbelieving smile, he knew deep down that even if Jamie did survive the blast he would be in imminent danger, as The Heron was still alive and probably waiting to ambush Jamie.

****

Lola was still squirming and Flapper was still building up the courage to try his crazy plan. He reached over to the nearest piece of rubble he could find without making any noise or having to stand up for too long. He grasped at a tennis ball sized piece and drew his wing back ready to throw it at the altar behind him, far away from where he was lying.

The Heron had now tied Lola to one of the pews, using a sash from the confessional boxes curtain and was getting ready to use the Ripper on her.

Frank raised the Ripper, pressed the trigger and nothing. Once again the Ripper had failed to fire.

"What's the matter Frank, what have you done now? You imbecile."

"I don't know Heron I can't make it out. It's counting down, I think from a hundred."

"Let me have a look Wally brain."

Heron grabbed at the Ripper. There was a small digital display on top of it which had the words: **RECHARGING**

PLEASE WAIT in luminescent green with the countdown underneath.

"Oh great, now what?" Frank said under his breath.

Flapper smirked at Frank, and saw this as his opportunity to create the distraction. He raised his wing and threw the fallen piece of rubble hard at the vestry door in the back of the church. The rubble hit so hard against the old oak door that it caused it to splinter slightly from the impact.

Both Frank and the Heron bolted upright, startled by the noise.

"Frank, go and check it out," The Heron demanded.

Reluctantly Frank put the Ripper down on a nearby pew and hopped over to the vestry door where he saw a small pile of stone chippings and an impact mark on the door. He stood there for a while puzzled at the mark, scratching his beak with his long sharp claws.

Flapper crept out from the cushions like a young rabbit emerging from his den for the first time in the spring. Wearily he crept towards the Heron, peering back over his wings to see if Frank had figured out where the rubble had come from. Flapper sniggered again when he saw him still standing there scratching his beak.

Flapper snapped his head back to see the Heron staring into his eyes. He fell backwards, startled by the Heron.

"Ha, thought you could get the better of me did you?" The Heron said, cackling at Flapper.

Flapper jumped up to meet the Heron. Unfortunately, the Heron was quite a lot taller than Flapper, but Flapper was stronger and faster. Flapper stretched out his wings to reveal his impressive wingspan to try to intimidate The Heron.

"Is that supposed to scare me?" The Heron held aloft Lola and grabbed at the nearest thing he could find which happened to be a bible, and went to throw it at Flapper's head when suddenly he stopped mid throw.

There was a crash at the main doors, then another, and another.

Then suddenly the doors crashed open, knocking a small table over and sending a box of leaflets cascading to the floor. Amongst the leaflets and light dust shower stood a small silhouette of a disgruntled, dusty and bruised frog breathing rather heavily.

"I...I Don't believe it, it can't be, but you're dead," The Heron said in amazement.

"Believe it or not Heron, you will be going to jail!"

Jamie had managed to activate his sudden impact safety device on his utility belt just before the devastating blast in HQ. This device created a small bubble shaped force field, stopping the walls from caving in on Jamie and forming a small cave just large enough for him to escape.

As Jamie emerged from the small hole, he was faced with a soppy looking dog and what looked to be a small starling straddled across the dog's back.

The dog lowered its head to Jamie and a small voice spoke, "Hop on, I'm here to help."

Unconvinced, Jamie backed away from the drooling slobbery mess that nearly resembled a ferocious animal if weren't for the drool hanging down like a set of shoelaces.

"Really, I know where Lola and your bird have gone. The Heron has them," Shifty said, a bit more reassuringly this time.

Jamie looked deep into Shifty's eyes.

Satisfied with the uncomfortable stare he had given Shifty he proceeded to climb up onto Mr. Drool and let the unlikely allies lead him to the Heron, Lola, and Flapper.

Jamie stepped forward from the door and slammed it shut behind him. Startled by Jamie's big entrance, Heron dropped Lola to the floor and tried to launch himself up into the vaulted roof and on to the rafters, but failed when his leg got trapped in a vented grill between the pews.

Jamie threw himself at Lola, furiously grabbing at her binds. When the binds came free, Jamie flung Lola full force onto Flappers back. Flapper grimaced as she grabbed at his feathers, nearly pulling them straight out of his back.

She hung there for dear life as Flapper took a run-up down the aisle towards the front doors next to Jamie.

He shot through the window he had broken through earlier. Splinters of glass showered the grass below the window and his wing tips clipped the sides of the window frame, leaving some of his feathers behind in the splintered timber frame.

Jamie launched himself at one of the columns near the centre of the entrance, swinging and twisting, ascending the column into the rafters of the vaulted roof.

The Heron frantically tried to free his leg from one of the pews when he felt the rush of air as Jamie jumped into the rafters. Jamie sat, perched on a dusty rafter and laughing at the sight of the Heron in such distress.

"GRRRR just you wait, Jamie," The Heron growled.

Frank saw The Heron struggling as well and again had to smile to himself at such a sight.

A Heron flapping around in circles is quite a strange thing indeed because their wings are so out of proportion to the rest of their bodies.

Frank hopped over to The Heron who by now was becoming extremely angry at his own predicament.

"Do you require some assistance Heron?" Frank asked sarcastically.

"Just get your feathery behind over here," The Heron demanded.

Jamie by now was wondering whether or not to just walk away and leave them to it or jump down and help the Heron himself, either way the predicament made Jamie smile. He grabbed at his communicator and dialed the temporary headquarters below the church, when The Heron snapped free all of a sudden and took off like a rocket, leaving a cloud of dust and Frank holding his beak to stop the dust cloud setting his allergies off.

The Heron landed on Jamie's perch only to find he had already moved. Jamie had anticipated the Heron's move and scuttled as fast as his little green legs could carry him on to a neighbouring rafter.

"Agent J," The Heron shouted at Jamie.

Suddenly they all stopped to hear a softly spoken female voice counting down "5-4-3-2-1 Ripper is fully charged."

"Perfect," Frank thought to himself.

Frank grabbed for the Ripper. He had goose bumps when he grabbed the stock. A loud whirring noise started and a cooling fan kicked in. He could feel the power vibrating through the trigger. Frank aimed the Ripper somewhere near Jamie's position.

Jamie scuttled again, leaping from rafter to rafter, trying to get out of the way of Frank's aim and stay ahead of The Heron at the same time.

Frank fired off a bolt of light at one of the rafters Jamie had been resting on, causing a small wormhole around the rafter. Wood splintered and dust swirled around in the vortex and part of the rafter fizzled off into the swirling hole.

The church roof began to creak, and then groan from the missing rafter. A roof tile slid off and smashed near the entrance to the church.

Jamie popped his head up for a second and saw The Heron bounding towards him. He fumbled in his utility belt for his laser cutter to use it on The Heron.

The Heron was nearly caught up in the Ripper's wormhole when it hit. He felt the pull of the vortex on his feathers as he jumped clear towards Jamie.

"FRANK!" The Heron shouted, followed by, "WHAT ARE YOU DOING, NOT ME, GET J!"

"SORRY!" Frank shouted back before letting another bolt of light go from the Ripper. This one struck nearer to Jamie causing the same effect as before, but this time the wormhole started directly under one of the main rafter joints, causing the church roof to buckle slightly.

Jamie had to get out of there before the whole place collapsed around him. The Heron, again nearly sucked into oblivion, had the same thought as Jamie - get out whilst the going was good. The vortexes formed by the Ripper were not going away this time. They were beginning to link together, forming one big vortex at the centre of the church.

Jamie leapt again from the rafters and grabbed at a long decorative sash hanging down the back wall above the altar of the church. He slid down the length of the sash, burning his small green hands from the friction as he picked up speed.

Frank turned suddenly to see Jamie running towards him, laser primed and aimed for the Ripper. With no telling what could happen to the Ripper or anybody near it Jamie fired his laser, heating up its casing and melting the aluminium surrounding the cooling fan.

Frank dropped the Ripper to the ground as the heat became too intense for him to hold. He turned and started towards the entrance of the church. Jamie carried on trying to destroy the Ripper.

The Ripper was now glowing white hot and hurt your eyes if you looked directly at it. It became so hot the surrounding oak pews lacquer began to blister and boil.

The Heron tried to stop Jamie from destroying the Ripper and out of pure greed, he flew down to grab at it, to take it out of harm's way. But it was already too late. The Ripper burst into bright blue flames and the air around it began to swell and distort from the heat. Jamie dropped his laser cutter and bolted to the church door, not looking back to see where The Heron was or whether the Ripper would explode, self-preservation kicked in and he wanted to live.

Suddenly a shock wave blasted from the Ripper, clearing the centre of the church. Splintered wood and glass exploded everywhere. The Heron tried to duck down away from the blast but was knocked down from the awesome force of the shock wave.

Tall blue flames shot up out of the Ripper blocking the Heron's escape, the air around him began to swell and twist into a vortex like nothing he had ever seen before. Like a powerful electro magnet, the vortex was drawing pews and rafters into it. The rafters began to creak and groan under the strain of the pull of the large vortex that had now formed at the centre of the church.

The vortex moved slowly, drawn to the Ripper's power.

Jamie reached for the front door of the church and his fingertips caught the face of the door making him grimace as they scraped the splintering wood.

He scurried to his feet once again, turned, and saw the Ripper swell as if it was alive or even breathing. Jamie, a bit terrified by this, scrambled again for the door, this time grabbing for the underneath. Getting a firm grip, he yanked as hard as he could to pull the door open.

He opened the door just enough for him to squeeze through as the Ripper imploded into a massive wormhole, ripping pews out of the ground and folding them in two as if they were made of paper rather than solid oak.

Frank quickly followed behind Jamie, shoving the door open even more.

He pulled at Jamie to try to gain a bit more ground between him and the church but with no luck. Jamie's legs were too powerful even for a bald eagle to hold back. Jamie dived behind the nearest gravestone he could get to and hugged it for dear life.

Just then, The Heron appeared at the doorway looking terrified, clinging on for all he was worth but the Ripper had him. It dragged him back towards the centre of its swirling vortex. The vortex was now so large it was consuming the whole church from the inside out.

The Heron shouted at Frank for help but he had already taken off and was too far from the church to be able to hear The Heron's calls.

However, Jamie could hear the Heron shouting for Frank and decided that no matter what he had done he didn't deserve to be lost forever in the vortex. Justice must be served.

Jamie stepped away from the gravestone and walked towards The Heron to help him.

Parts of the roof had now fallen into the vortex. The walls started to shudder. Splinters of wood the size of cricket bats were flying off the oak clad vestry walls. Jamie grabbed hold of Heron's feathery hand, trying to pull him away from the engulfing vortex. He struggled and struggled, pulling with all his might, but the vortex had such a hold of The Heron that it was pulling feathers from his back. Another part of the roof collapsed into the vortex, smothering the two in dust and small chunks of rubble. The vortex was so big now it was bigger than a double decker bus.

****

Flapper and Lola arrived at the destroyed headquarters, finding Red and Cod standing over a frog shaped hole containing a rather squashed rucksack.

"Red, Jamie's alive," Lola screamed.

"I knew it," Red replied quietly and with some relief. "Where is he then?"

"At the old church in Colgate," Flapper replied, fighting for breath.

"Lola, wait here with Red," Flapper demanded, still fighting for breath.

"Where are you going?" Lola asked.

"I'm going back for Jamie."

"Be careful, Flapper."

"Don't worry Lola, I can take care of myself."

"Somehow I think you can, Flapper," Lola replied.

Flapper left a small dust cloud behind when he thrust his wings into the ground for a little extra lift.

Cod put a rather wet and slimy fin around Lola's shoulders, which made Lola shiver, "Flapper will get him back safely Lola, don't you worry."

Cod's usual booming voice had softened slightly, making Lola and Red feel uneasy and surprised by his change in tone. This didn't happen all that often. You would have more chance of getting a pay rise rather than full on arm hugging sympathy.

****

The Ripper's swirling wormhole suddenly became even stronger, ripping a large flint wall from its foundations. The Heron's grip slipped off the door. Jamie's grip was slipping too. He was plucking feathers as he tried to grab at the Heron's hands again. Just then, Flapper appeared from nowhere and helped Jamie to try to pull The Heron to safety.

Flapper took hold of Jamie's body and pulled with all his might, but the Ripper's vortex was now so powerful that it was dragging in everything, even the floor beneath itself. The Heron knew it was too late for them to try to save him. Jamie could feel The Heron's grip loosen.

"Heron hold on, don't let go," Jamie demanded.

The Heron looked into Jamie's eyes. He gave an enigmatic smile, winked and then let go. He was slowly sucked into the vortex just as the roof collapsed, smothering the vortex and the remains of the Ripper.

There was a big crash and an ear splitting splintering boom as the vortex closed in on itself. Smaller and smaller the vortex closed in, crushing large stone blocks and ripping smaller chunks of earth from the ground. Then there was nothing, just a few stone columns that shuddered for a moment but quickly settled. The door that The Heron had gripped so tightly was still standing, swinging gently back and forth.

Flapper and Jamie stepped back from the door in awe of what had just happened to The Heron and the church.

"Oh my god, and what the hell?" Jamie tried to speak but was too dumbfounded to know what to say or do.

Flapper's mouth gaped wide in amazement.

Lola called Jamie's communicator. "Jamie, are you ok?"

Jamie took his communicator out of his utility belt and answered, "I don't know if I am or not Lola."

Flapper grabbed the device off Jamie. "The Heron has gone. He got sucked into a wormhole the same as we thought happened with the dogs."

"Oh my, are you and Jamie ok?" asked Lola.

Jamie looked at Flapper with dismay and decided not to respond.

"Let's head back to Lola at Tilgate," Jamie said to Flapper.

Flapper agreed with Jamie and lowered his left wing for Jamie to climb on board.

Once settled Flapper took a gentler run up this time around, Jamie lying flat on Flappers back, exhausted from the episode at the church.

They flew over the destroyed headquarters at Tilgate.

"Jamie look! Look down there," Flapper tilted his left wing and circled around the newly formed hole next to Jamie's lake.

There were clean up teams at the site trying to make good of the new hole and salvage as much CCTV footage as they could from the burnt out shell of the old headquarters. Jamie could see Lola dancing around, waving her arms around and calling Jamie and Flapper down to a hero's welcome.

Red, overjoyed by the safe return of his best pal jumped in absolute glee. Flapper landed next to a smouldering hawthorn bush at the edge of the lake and turned to see if the officer's mess was still intact. To his surprise it was, and there were his friends tucking into cool chilled strawberry milk drinks.

Jamie jumped down next to Flapper and said, "Flapper, go and join your buddies. I think I need to see my mate Red."

Flapper patted Jamie on the back and gave an approving smile as he wandered over to the bar.

Jamie pulled himself together and stopped for a moment before walking over to a very excited channel catfish, and an even more ecstatic Lola.

"You're ok Jamie. I can't believe you managed to survive, first the blast at headquarters and then the Ripper exploding. You really must be bullet proof. Either that or just really lucky," Lola exclaimed.

Before Jamie could answer Lola's comment he heard, "Jamie me old green pal, I always knew you would make it."

"Red, thanks old buddy. I thought I was toast back there as well, if it hadn't been for Flapper."

"Lola, where are you?" Jamie turned around, looking for her.

"Ah, there you are sweetheart."

Lola was shocked at his comment. "Jamie, I'm so glad you're alive but please don't call me sweetheart."

Jamie tilted his head to one side before grabbing at Lola and giving her a massive squeeze.

Lola wasn't usually one for this kind of thing but considering all they had been through she obliged just this once. Jamie and Lola stayed cuddling, feeling safe and warm but still slimy. They are frogs of course.

Cod called Red on his PDA, "Red I need you to come over to Colgate at once and help me here. There is a situation."

"What, already? Oh, do you need a cup of tea sir?" Red cheekily replied.

"No, I have a problem with some rats, dear boy."

"Ok Boss, on my way."

"Sorry Jamie, Cod has called. I need to shoot over to Colgate."

"Red we'll meet you there. I need to debrief the old fish anyway."

Lola released her tight grip from Jamie and headed towards the officer's mess. Jamie followed closely.

****

At the edge of a clearing, watching from under a hawthorn bush there were big bulbous fiery red eyes with pupils growing larger by the second as they watched Jamie's every move. A large hairy hand grabbed at a passing dragonfly. Its eyes oozed a yellow gooey liquid when they popped from the bite of the crazed squirrel like creature.

The thing carried on watching as Flapper, Jamie, and Lola walked into the officer's mess.

FINAL - STRANGE PLANETS

A cloud of dust settled around his grey feathery hands. He shivered from the cold of the Ripper's vortex. His head was pounding from the immense pressure emitted from the wormhole, travelling from one dimension and into another.

The Heron sat on a pile of church rubble wondering where he was and to what time or where he had been taken, or even if there were any other beings?

It was quite clear to him that there was enough air to breathe in the atmosphere. Otherwise, he would be dead already. He could hear the wind rustling through strange orange trees and what he thought sounded like birds chattering to each other but could not be quite sure.

He decided to stand up and take a look around this new world. His legs trembled as he tried to stand, still weak from the incredible travel through the wormhole. He steadied himself, shook out his feathers, and stretched both his neck and wings. There was an almighty crack from his neck and then silence all around him as if someone had pressed the mute button on a remote control.

The bird noises had stopped, even the rustling had stopped. The Heron started to panic a little. He scanned his eyes around the strange looking trees and prickly green grass. Raising his head up to, the sky he did not believe what his eyes saw. A greenish coloured cloud passed overhead blocking his view of the marvel overhead.

There were planets in view and several small suns. One planet was so large it took up most of the horizon whilst others were quite a lot smaller than the giant planet. The biggest planet looked a lot like earth with blue oceans and green land dotted around its surface. The others had swirling patterns on their surfaces, a bit like a child's kaleidoscope.

He was wrapped up in the amazing skyline, so wrapped up he hadn't noticed the strange little inhabitants of the planet gathering around him. They looked a lot like a bunny rabbit but with big bulbous eyes and enormous ears shaped like a satellite dish. The nose was distended and the tail was about the same length as a rat's tail, the fur covered most of the body but left a scaly underbelly and only part of the tail had fur on it, as the rest was scaled until the end where it had a small egg shaped end made of solid bone. They were green in colour, with a darker green tiger stripe pattern so they easily blended in with the surrounding environment of long spiky grass.

The Heron turned his neck slowly. His head followed and tilted toward a heavy breathing noise below him.

"Well, at least they look friendly. I come in peace," Heron said, loudly but nervously.

Suddenly a thousand ears appeared from nowhere, then a thousand more. Heron gulped at the sheer number of creatures surrounding him. What he didn't see was that just over the brow of a prickly hill was a larger version of these super bunnies. This was the mum, the dad followed in her shadow. He was slightly smaller but massive all the same.

Heron's mouth dropped open as the parents arrived. The earth beneath Heron's feet was shuddering from the weird bunnies leaps and bounds. With every bound from their parents, the smaller things bounced as well. The parents really were very big and bulky. Their bones were solid with a natural steel coating. The fur down the line of the back had metal spikes buried amongst the strands.

The bird like noise started again and he knew it was coming from the small rabbit like creatures. There weren't any birds on this planet, only little green monsters.

The heron flapped his wings, trying to launch up and away but some of the green things had grabbed a strong hold of his feet, pulling him back down to the surface. The

Heron blacked out for a few seconds and then woke to see big huge teeth biting down on him.

The female of the two had him in a motherly hold in her teeth, carrying him back to their warren. The green rabbit like creatures had never seen a Heron before. Now they had a new playmate and The Heron, if he could find a way back to earth had a new army! He cackled a sinister laugh as the little green monsters carried him away.

Jamie Pond will return!

LOOK OUT FOR MORE TITLES IN
THE ADVENTURES OF JAMIE POND SERIES

COMING SOON

2017

JAMIE POND IN RISE OF THE THUNDER RABBIT

2018

JAMIE POND IN RISE OF THE DOOMSDAY SQUIRREL

2019

JAMIE POND IN RISE OF THE RAT KING

2020

SECRET AGENT LOLA

2021

DOUBLE AGENT STARRING SECRET AGENT LOLA

By D.P. Hall

ABOUT THE AUTHOR

David writes children's books in his spare time and works full time as a busy and accomplished construction manager for lifting operations.

David was born in 1976 and grew up in Yateley, Surry. He moved to West Sussex in 1986 to complete his schooling and lives there now with his wife and their three children.

With a vivid imagination and a keen eye for art, David, draws all the illustrations for his books including the front and back covers.

He started writing in 2009, on this his first book Jamie Pond In Rise Of The Heron, and has plans to write three more books in the Jamie Pond Series.

Jamie Pond In Rise Of The Thunder Rabbit being the next in the series.

David is determined to make a full time career change and be all he can be in writing children's books and on the odd occasion maybe a book for the bigger kids.

Printed in Poland
by Amazon Fulfillment
Poland Sp. z o.o., Wrocław